SHE WAS GUILTY
OF BEING TOO BEAUTIFUL . . .

In 1840 a woman was lost in a world ruled by men.
Sabrina's hot, rebellious spirit had freed her from the
tyranny of her papa, but it could not free the dazzling
red-haired beauty from her own confused emotions.
When she met Johnny Graham and saw the scorn in his
eyes, she was plunged once more into a complicated web
of deceit and treachery. How could she prove to him
that the scandalous accusations of the past against her
virtue were false? How could she ever make him believe
that she loved only him?

DANCING HILL

Sheila Holland

PLAYBOY PRESS
PAPERBACKS

CHAPTER ONE

They left Cambridge at eight o'clock on a fine spring morning, jolting along the unfamiliar London road with that constant sense of anticipation which any journey into the unknown brings. Sabrina, having been fortunate enough to procure a corner seat, stared out of the window at the flat green water meadows, springy underfoot in dry weather but still sodden with March rain today, the thirsty willows trailing sere fingers to the grass. Even the unhappiness of much of their life in Cambridge could not detract from that calm, cool beauty, she thought, gazing back at the town as the coach swung round a corner, giving a last glimpse of creamy stone and fretted towers before they vanished again.

Images of other years came and went in her mind: summer afternoons on the Backs, the dimpled water running golden through her fingers as they punted under the willows. Why were the summers of childhood so golden, she wondered? And what happened to summer as one grew up?

The coach lurched violently, wheels grating, the whip of the coachman cracking as he shouted to the horses, and the travelers within were jolted back and forth, bumping into one another.

"Gracious heavens," muttered a thin lady in rustling gray, her eyes nervously rolling upward. She smiled at Sabrina as their eyes met. "I am such a poor traveler. I wish they would not drive at such a speed."

"They are forced to it, ma'am," interrupted a portly gentleman, putting down his *Times* to glare at her. "They must keep to their time! Time is valuable! I have an important engagement in London this afternoon—I must not be late. When we have a reliable railway service in this country, business will boom, boom, ma'am!"

"Railway!" moaned the thin lady, clutching at her mittens.

"Yes, ma'am. After all, this is the year 1841. We are not living in the Dark Ages. Trade needs speed." And pulling out his large gold watch, he clicked open the case, nodding with satisfaction, "On time!" And he retired once more behind his newspaper.

Sabrina smiled sympathetically at the distraught lady in gray, then leaned back and looked at her sister, Charity, sitting bolt upright beside her, hands folded precisely in her lap.

For once, she thought with pleasure, Charity had color in her cheeks.

Normally Charity's coloring was doused by the somber clothes she wore. Small, slight, sexless, in her confining black gown, her cheeks held a faint flush of excitement today. The blue eyes, widely spaced and childlike, held wistful appeal, but the shyness that afflicted her made her unable to look directly at a stranger, so that it was only those who knew her well who ever saw that sweet, gentle glance.

From beneath her black bonnet strayed limp strands of very pale golden hair. Her mouth had patience molded into every curve, the patience born of bitter experience.

Watching her now, Sabrina felt a familiar prick of anger. Papa has much to answer for, she thought, her eyes smoldering, and then, with incredulity, remembered how Charity had wept the day their father died.

Sabrina had gone to her, arms outstretched, ready to comfort her, although herself unable to feel any grief for the stern, unbending man who had made of their lives a grim test of endurance. She had expected Charity to weep, knowing her gentleness, but the depth of Charity's grief had surprised her.

"Poor Papa," the girl had wept, leaning against her. "Oh, Sabrina, poor Papa . . ."

And Sabrina, stroking her hair and murmuring softly, had marveled. For Charity had been the chief victim of his particular brand of icy cruelty. Yielding and affectionate, she had quivered, white-faced, under the biting irony, the sarcasm, the rebuffs administered by a clever tongue that sought to wound and always succeeded with her.

With his elder daughter, Sabrina, he had more difficulty. Her hot, rebellious spirit freed her from his tyranny quite early in her life. She could face him out, eyes contemptuous, and he always turned away first.

The sisters could not have been less alike. Sabrina's hair was a rich red-gold, thick and shining, falling to her waist in gleaming coils when she loosed it. Her finely modeled face blazed with vitality, blue-green eyes changing with every mood, her skin a smooth creamy white, her mouth red and passionate. In every look and gesture, impatience, warmth and energy pulsed visibly.

After their father's death, they had found a miniature of their mother among his papers and, from it, discovered the source of Sabrina's coloring and nature. Vivacious, gay, she had smiled out at them, even the shape of her eyes an echo of Sabrina. And both girls had stared curiously, wishing they could remember their mother.

That morning a solicitor arrived at the house with a letter from their mother's brother, Matthew Wilton, offering them a home. Sabrina, who had planned to take a position as a governess, had been reluctant to accept this kindness, but Charity, in terror at the idea of earning her own bread, had leaped at the chance, and Sabrina was persuaded to accompany her.

"I have always longed to see Ambreys!" Charity had pleaded, clinging to her hands as if she were drowning. "Do you not remember when Papa told us of it?" And her eyes had filled with tears again, "Poor dear Papa!"

Poor dear Papa, indeed! Sabrina's lips tightened, but she had a brief flash of nostalgia, even so, remembering the day their father had shown them a water-color painted by their mother, of a square white Georgian house set among elms and massive, frilled oaks, with green lawns stretching down to a small lake fringed with dark reeds from which a wild goose rose, neck stretched in flight.

"Ambreys," Papa had said, lips wry. "Your

mother was born there. The house is named after some earthwork fortifications in the forest near Epping, an ancient British camp. There is a legend that Boadicea camped there on the night before her last battle. They call it Ambresbury Banks now, but the old name was Ambreys, and when the house was built, your great-great grandfather took the name for his new house because he was an amateur antiquarian."

They had eagerly asked after their mother's family, but he had turned away. "Run along to your nurse! I am busy."

Typical of Papa, she thought, to speak with interest of a British camp and yet refuse to tell them of their mother's family, a subject which interested them a great deal more.

The watercolor had given her an image of her mother's childhood that had remained with her. Gracious, sunny, filled with affection, it had comforted her in the night when she was unhappy. There had been a feeling of warmth in the painting. She had sensed that it was painted with nostalgic yearning and had wondered about her dead mother and whether she, too, had been the butt of Papa's bitter sarcasm.

And so, when Charity pleaded with her to go to Ambreys, she had been drawn to the thought of that painted image of lost happiness and had wavered.

"We will be together," Charity had pointed out. "I could not bear it if we were separated. I do not mind how hard I have to work, but I hate the idea of being away from you, with strangers in a strange place. You know you hated it when you went to London."

Sabrina had flushed hotly and glanced away. "I have never told you so," she evaded.

"You did not need to do so. I knew. Your letters were like the letters of a stranger, and then you came home suddenly, without warning, and looking quite ill. I did not ask you any questions because I knew how I would hate being governess to three spoiled children. I thought it best to forget the whole episode."

Sabrina glanced at her from beneath her lashes, curiously, her expression wry.

"Say you will come, Sabrina," Charity pressed. "It is very kind of Uncle Matthew. And think! We have never seen our cousins. I wonder if they will like us?"

"We shall be poor relations, dependent upon their charity," Sabrina warned. "You do not know how hard that can be, Charity."

"They sound too kind to remind us of it. I feel certain we will be happy at Ambreys. I have wanted to see it for so long, and we shall never have another chance like this. If we are not happy after all, we can always leave."

With a sigh, Sabrina had yielded and been engulfed in a hug. But her doubts had not been quieted, and now, closing her eyes, she wished she possessed the gift of second sight and could know what awaited them at Ambreys.

It was late in the afternoon when they arrived at the Cock Hotel in Epping, and were met by their uncle's coachman.

Sabrina was relieved by his courtesy as he handed them up into the carriage and folded the steps up before closing the door. She had learned, on her brief excursion to London, that servants always reflect the attitudes of their employers.

Charity, huddling in the corner, said faintly, "Oh, dear . . ."

"What now?" Sabrina asked indulgently.

"I feel sick."

"If you are sick, I shall never forgive you," Sabrina warned, mock-severely.

"Oh, Sabrina, I am so glad you are here! If I had to go alone, I am sure it would kill me!"

"You would survive," said Sabrina dryly, but her eyes anxiously noted her sister's pallor and the trembling of her hands.

They drove through narrow country lanes, under tall hedgerows, black and leafless in this month but busy with birds. The sun shone a pale golden light over the fields. Above them ran a seemingly endless stretch of forest, the trees just beginning to show that misty green that is almost a trick of light in spring, but slowly becomes the reality of leaf and bud as the days go by.

"Epping Forest," said Sabrina. "I wonder if we will be able to visit it one day. I would like to see Ambresbury Banks."

They began to pass small cottages, with neat gardens, clipped hedges and white-painted gates. Some women, gossiping by the pump, turned to curtsey as the carriage passed, their faces curious.

Then came a new, red brick school, with the date 1841 over the door, the open yard in front enclosed with iron railings. Beside it stood a cottage built of the same brick, the windows bare, the small garden dug over but showing no tree or plant.

"They must have been built very recently," said Sabrina. "The village must be quite large to support such a school."

Between the cottage and the church lay a meadow hedged with hawthorn in which some horses grazed, and some little girls were running about in the churchyard, laughing.

The church was of gray stone but had a wooden tower, which gave it an odd appearance, and the graves were neatly trimmed and clear of moss. Beyond it lay a large house, which they guessed to be the vicarage, the walls covered with a dark green ivy. A window was open upstairs, and a maid in white cap shook a duster out of the window, then stared down at the carriage. A woman in a dark green gown came to the front door and called sharply to the little girls, who ran through a gate in the churchyard wall. They went into the house, pointing at the carriage, with bright, interested faces, their voices carrying to Sabrina.

Then they had passed out of the village and turned into a wide drive, under stone gates topped by carved birds, of indistinguishable origin, and drove down between lines of beech trees, their boughs moving, creaking in the wind, bare of leaves, but tipped with sticky black buds.

They emerged on a graveled drive that ran round the front of the house. It faced them, white, sturdy, elegantly practical, a portico of tapering pillars giving classic grace to the nicely proportioned ranks of flat windows.

As the carriage halted, the front door was flung open, and out stepped a slight, stooping figure, his balding head bare, peering down at them, waving forward the servants who stood behind.

The carriage door opened; they were helped down and found themselves facing their uncle. His skin was brown from exposure to wind and weather, and he smiled faintly as he said, "Welcome to Ambreys, my dears." His pale blue eyes skimmed from one to the other. "Your aunt is waiting in the drawing room."

Sabrina curtsied and began a polite speech of gratitude.

He interrupted, "Nonsense, nonsense. Your mother was my only sister. The quarrel between us was not of my making, and although I would not wish to speak ill of the dead, I would like you to know that we would have seen you here at Ambreys long ago if your father had been less difficult. Still, that is past. Now you are here, and I want you to regard Ambreys as your home."

Charity, worn out by the journey and the emotion of the moment, burst into tears.

Sabrina, seeing her uncle flinch with the embarrassment peculiar to men faced by feminine vapors, put an arm round her and said, "My sister is overwrought, sir. The journey . . ."

"Of course," he said hurriedly, "perhaps we should go into the house."

They followed him into the high-ceilinged hall and then into another room papered with fashion-

able flowery wall covering, where they found their
aunt in the position of one who has assumed an attitude and is determined to hold it.

"Maria, my dear, here they are at last . . ."

His wife turned her head, a polite smile on her
lips, her plump face composed for a word of welcome, but as her eyes fell on Sabrina, freezing, black
eyes hard as jet.

Sabrina had seen that look before and received it
calmly, yet with a sinking heart.

"This is Sabrina," said Uncle Matthew cheerfully,
"pretty as a picture, isn't she?"

"Very pretty," said Aunt Maria heavily, and her
glance shot sideways at the young man seated nearby
who was leaning forward with parted lips and admiring eyes, staring at Sabrina.

"My son, Tom, lately returned from Oxford,"
Uncle Matthew told them.

Tom sprang up, smiling eagerly, and came to take
Sabrina's hand and press it with warmth. He was
about twenty, with fair hair and coloring, his chin
and mouth betraying a weakness of character. "I
say, Sabrina, that is an unusual name! Where did
your parents find it? I never heard it before."

"Milton," she answered, amused, "it is the Latin
name for the River Severn. Milton used it in a
poem."

"Oh, that Milton," he said, his face falling, "not
much of a reader, don't you know."

"Tom," cried Aunt Maria sharply, "ring for
Pearton."

With a resentful glance, he obeyed, and Uncle
Matthew brought forward his daughter, Louisa, a

short dumpy girl, with flat brown hair swept up in a bun, black eyes and a discontented expression. Every few moments she threw a nervous glance at her mother, then hurriedly muttered some polite word about the weather, their journey or the pleasures of London.

The servant arrived to show them to their rooms, and Tom walked with them to the door, gazing ardently at Sabrina as he held it open.

"Tom," his mother called, and he hurried back to her. Sabrina heard her say anxiously, "Oh, I hope you have learned your lesson, Tom. We do not want a repetition of your Oxford folly. Matthew, speak to the boy . . ."

Tom growled something about being nagged to death, and his father said sternly, "Now, Tom, listen to your mother . . ."

Then the door shut, and Sabrina hurried after the servant and Charity.

Their rooms were pleasant. There were flowers beside the beds and fresh warm water in the china washbasins. Pearton, a tall, angular woman of forty, spoke politely and seemed disposed to be friendly. When she had left them, Sabrina sank onto a chair and sighed in relief.

"Well, here we are," she said.

"Oh, they seem so kind," Charity said. "I believe they really want us."

Sabrina glanced at her but said nothing to disabuse her of this belief. She knew instinctively that had she been plain and dull, her aunt would have been much kinder. Mothers with impressionable sons did not welcome the intrusion of pretty, possibly ambitious girls into their home. She guessed from Tom's attentions that he was prone to falling in love, and presumably, from his mother's remarks, with ineligible girls.

She rose and walked to the dressing table and stared at herself with exasperation. What was there in the combination of red hair and green eyes that made men look sideways and women tighten their lips and speak so coldly?

And, remembering another household into which she had come, ignorant, trusting, unaware of herself, she shivered.

This time, she thought, I am warned. I know the pitfalls and can avoid them.

Aloud, she said, "Lie down and rest, you look quite white. I will be next door, remember. Call if you need me." And, having kissed her sister, went softly out of the room.

She sat on the window seat of her own room and gazed out over the rolling lawns, thinking of quite a different setting, the narrow foggy streets of London, where she had spent some months, three years earlier.

She had been recommended for the position as governess in the household of a famous London physician, Sir Lucas Graham, by a friend of her father, and had gone to London with high hopes and a total innocence of the world.

Sir Lucas had three children, all girls, but their mother had no great faith in education and was in the habit of excusing them from their lessons in order that they might sit in the drawing room with her and entertain her callers, or drive out with her in the park. Sir Lucas's nephew, John Graham, was working with him and lived in the house. Lady Graham had taken an immediate dislike to Sabrina, suspecting her red hair on sight, and, lonely and isolated, the girl spent too many hours in her tiny attic bedroom, reading and sewing.

When one day she met John Graham in the park, her loneliness made her respond more warmly than she would have done to his offer of a visit to the City to see the famous churches. She knew how her father would regard such behavior, but she was so weary of her own company, and John Graham was so charming.

Their friendship grew rapidly, deepened, became love, and at length Johnny asked her to marry him. "I have no money nor any prospects of any beside what I shall earn," he told her softly. "My family estate is entailed on my brother. But we shall not go in want, Sabrina."

Their relationship had been kept hidden from his family, more for her sake than for his, and she, with this secret too valuable to share, had not even written to Charity about him. And so it was with anxiety that she replied: "Your uncle will not like it!"

"Why not? There is no family property involved, and I am of age. Don't look so anxious, my love. They cannot stop us."

That evening Lady Graham dined out, and Sir Lucas and Johnny were engaged with a very wealthy patient, so Sabrina dined alone. Halfway through the meal, Sir Lucas arrived and joined her. She saw that he was somewhat elevated and, with some uneasiness, watched as he drank copiously of the wine served.

"My Lady is very satisfied with her new son," he said, raising his glass. "I was toasted a dozen times by her husband, the Baronet. A good evening, my dear, a good evening."

She hoped that he would remain in the dining room when she left, but he followed her into the drawing room and sank into a comfortable chair, laughing stupidly. "Damned hot in here!" he said, pulling at his collar.

"Shall I have the window opened?" she asked, going to pull the bell rope.

As she passed his chair, he reached up suddenly, grinning, and pulled her down on his lap. "Pretty piece," he muttered, kissing her, his beard grazing her skin. She was so taken aback that for a moment she lay quiescent in his arms.

Then an outraged voice made him jerk up his head, the flush receding from his cheeks, leaving him pale.

"Lucas! How dare you? Oh, I knew it! I knew what was going on behind my back . . ."

Sabrina struggled to her feet, shivering in disgust and shock, and turned to face Lady Graham. Then her eyes widened as she saw Johnny, standing at his aunt's shoulder, his own face white and hard.

Lady Graham said hissingly, "You will leave this house, you little harlot. I knew what you were from the start. Coming here, seducing my husband . . ."

"No," Sabrina exclaimed desperately, her eyes on Johnny, "it is not true . . ." Her face was now as white as his, her voice full of appeal, but he turned away and went into the hall. She heard the front door bang, and her heart seemed to stop beating for a second, then anguish flooded in, and she shook with a pain that made her deaf to all the insults Lady Graham offered.

Somehow she packed her bags, caught the coach to Cambridge and made some explanation to her father for her sudden return. What she had said and how he had replied, she could not remember. Those days were blank to her, wiped out by her mind in an effort to protect her. The days had gone by, marked by fire as the pain burned higher, or empty, distinguished by a sameness of misery when her heart seemed numb.

Time had performed its usual miracle. The pain had grown less and less until she could now barely remember Johnny's face, but the humiliation had remained to gall her for a long time, and she was determined that here at Ambreys she would have no repetition of those events. Her cousin Tom must be put firmly in his place and kept there.

She leaned her head against the window, staring out at the distant blur of trees, the glint of water beyond the lawns, and a strange feeling of homecoming filled her. Ambreys, she said aloud. This is Ambreys.

It was foolish to feel elated, standing here, looking out on this calm scene. She had lived in beautiful surroundings before in Cambridge, where green turf, white stone and settled graciousness had formed the background of her childhood. But she had always felt shut out in Cambridge. She had not belonged. Only two classes of people fitted there: the young men who thronged the streets, talking loudly, and the fellows, stalking like blackbirds in the college grounds, the tutors and professors, gathering in state on Sundays to process into the chapel.

Harshly she reminded herself that here, too, she did not truly belong. She must give satisfaction as if she were a servant on trial. Pride burned in the back of her throat. I would rather earn my place, she thought, turning away from the seduction of that beautiful view. I should not have listened to Charity. I should have taken a position as a governess somewhere. Then I might feel some self-respect.

They dined that evening in a paneled room, the table groaning under the weight of the meal. Soup, game, fish, meat, cheese; one by one the courses came and went, and Sabrina kept a wary eye on her sister, knowing how small an appetite she had and how her digestion reacted to such a burden.

Their aunt seemed disposed to be kind to Charity, seeing no danger in her, and constantly pressed her to eat more, to Charity's scarcely repressed alarm.

After dinner they retired to the drawing room, where the men joined them shortly, to the relief of the women, for whom conversation was dragging intolerably. Even Aunt Maria looked relieved, although she threw a glance of warning at Tom as he made a bee-line for Sabrina's chair and sat down beside her.

"Do you ride, cousin? We have a decent stable. My sister has a nice little mare, only fifteen hands, but she never rides because she is terrified of falling off."

Louisa gave him a sullen look. "I broke my leg the last time I rode," she said.

"You are so lumpish, Louisa. You sit there like a

bag of oats jolting along." Tom turned his shoulder to her and gazed at Sabrina hopefully. "Will you come out with me before breakfast, cousin? I'll take you through the forest. Very pretty early in the morning, you know."

Aunt Maria stirred restlessly. "Your cousin will be too tired to ride tomorrow. She needs time to recover from her journey. Let her rest, Tom."

"Oh, Mama," he protested, "it will do her good!"

"Thank you, but I think I must refuse," Sabrina said quietly. "My aunt is right. I will be very stiff tomorrow. That coach ride was very tiring."

Tom's lower lip pouted. "Oh, I say," he muttered sulkily.

His mother looked sharply at Sabrina, who met her gaze calmly. "Perhaps you would like to see these water-color albums, my dear," she said slowly, "there are some here which were painted by your own Mama."

Sabrina rose eagerly, "I would, indeed, thank you, Aunt," she said.

Tom watched her with a scowl as she crossed to the sofa on which his mother sat, then he leaned back and poked at the carpet with his toe.

Aunt Maria took up the album and began to skim over the pages until she found a small landscape with a rose garden in the foreground and a distant view of the forest. "Here is one of your Mama's, my dear. She had some facility, I believe. Matthew often says she was very talented with her brush."

"I wish I had inherited it."

"You have her looks. I was quite surprised when I saw how like you were today." She looked sideways and added softly, "We are having a dinner party next week. I wonder if you would help me address the invitations tomorrow morning?"

"I should be glad to help," said Sabrina, sensing something behind the request.

"It is important to us that the party is a success. Among the guests are the parents of the young lady we hope will marry Tom."

"Indeed, Aunt?" Sabrina met her eyes firmly, and Aunt Maria watched her with some care.

"Sir George and Lady Colling," she added, smiling.

"They are neighbors of yours, perhaps?"

"Their house, Colling Grange, is two miles the other side of Epping. They have only one child, Charlotte, a pretty girl. She will inherit everything. There is no entail."

"You will be very busy with a wedding to arrange, Aunt," said Sabrina.

"Oh, Lady Colling will do most of that," said Aunt Maria, "but of course it is very exciting for us all. Such a pity poor little Vicky had to get measles. But Dr. Graham assures me that she will be up and about again long before June, which is when we hope to have the ceremony."

"Dr. Graham?" repeated Sabrina, her throat suddenly dry.

"Yes, our local doctor. Such a pleasant young man. His brother owns Dancing Hill; you may have heard of it. Elizabethan, and has a famous ballroom where Queen Elizabeth is supposed to have danced. A pair of her shoes is kept there in a glass case. A great many visitors call to see them." She turned the pages of the album idly. "Yes, but little good it has done poor Geoffrey Graham. He has contracted a disease of the lung and is gone to Switzerland, but I hear they do not expect him to recover, and so the estate will pass to our Dr. Graham."

"An ill wind, eh? Lucky Johnny Graham," Uncle Matthew chimed in, nodding.

Sabrina rose, her hands clenched at her side. "I . . . will you excuse me, Aunt? I am so tired . . ." She found it hard to speak at all, so fiercely did her heart beat against her breast, and she knew from their startled glances that something of her agitation must appear in her face.

Charity sprang to her side. "What is it? Are you ill?"

"No, no, just very tired," she said, her voice shaking.

"My poor child," said Aunt Maria, her hostility evaporating in sympathy. "Shall I come up with you? Do you feel faint?"

"No, indeed," protested Sabrina. "Excuse me . . ." And she hurried out of the room.

Upstairs, she flung herself on her bed, her hands to her forehead. A pulse beat wildly there, and her palms were damp with perspiration. Johnny—here? Did he know? Did he realize that she was coming to Ambreys? And if not, what would be his reaction? Would he tell her aunt of her disgrace in his uncle's house, of the scandal of her departure? She burned with anticipated humiliation as she lay there, twisting on the bed. Charity came and knocked at the door and called her name, but she lay still and did not answer.

The house lay silent all around her, full of strangers, and Sabrina wished herself a hundred miles away.

CHAPTER TWO

Next morning she woke with a clear head and a sense of cool defiance. Since she could not guess at Johnny's reaction to meeting her again, she must wait for the event with as much patience as she could muster, and, whatever happened, show an indifferent face to the world. She knew how little opportunity she would have to defend herself against the old charge. It was her word against that of Sir Lucas Graham and his wife. She was certain her aunt would prefer to believe the latter. Smiling grimly at her reflection in the mirror as she dressed, Sabrina cursed her own red hair and wished fervently that she had been born with mousy hair and a squint.

She spent the morning helping Aunt Maria with her list of guests for the dinner party. On gilt-edged cards they wrote the appropriate name in the space left by the engraver and tucked them into envelopes. Sabrina's fingers shook as she wrote Johnny's name on one card and then slowly addressed the envelope to Rose Tree Cottage, Ambresbury Village.

Her aunt, seeing her hesitation, the envelope lying in her palm, mistook the reason and explained, "That is the village, my dear. You came through it yesterday. This afternoon I will take you for a drive

25

through the lanes. I have to call at the schoolhouse to measure the windows."

Sabrina looked a question.

"Matthew made the biggest contribution to the school fund. He has always been in favor of education for the poor, although I do not see that it will do them much good. More likely to make them unsatisfied with their lives. But men have no common sense. Idealism is all very well, but it rarely works. He is on the school board, but of course it is myself who must see to the details of his precious school."

"It is not in use, yet? We thought it looked empty when we drove past."

"We have advertised for a schoolmistress, but had few replies, and none Matthew considered suitable. The salary is small, and this is a very remote area. I intend to furnish the house with some old furniture from Ambreys. It is perfectly good, but old-fashioned. There is no point in wasting money buying new."

"I imagine the Vicar's wife is some help to you, Aunt," said Sabrina idly.

Her aunt looked sourly at her. "Mrs. Fraser is a very managing woman. Far too busy in what does not concern her. Her family responsibilities do not seem to weigh too heavily upon her."

Sabrina suppressed a smile. "Has she a large family?"

"Large?" Aunt Maria leaned forward and spoke confidentially, "far too large, if you ask me. Four boys and two girls, and she is not yet thirty! When they are all at home, there is bedlam in the Vicarage.

Luckily, Mr. Fraser sends the boys to school so soon as they are seven."

After a prolonged luncheon, made uneasy for Sabrina by Tom's constant attempts to attract her notice, Aunt Maria suggested the two girls join her in a drive down to the schoolhouse. "We will kill two birds with one stone," she said, "introduce you to the neighborhood, and get those windows measured."

"I will accompany you, Mama," said Tom eagerly.

"There will not be room, Tom," she retorted, "we shall take the trap."

"Why not the carriage?" he asked, "and, you know, there is only room for two in the trap."

"It will take three quite comfortably, and we are none of us very large," his mother said firmly.

"Louisa would like to go," he said, nudging his sister.

She lifted her head sulkily. "No, I would not," she said, her lip protruding.

Tom gave her a furious, reproachful glare, but said no more. However, when they went out to seat themselves in the trap, they found Tom waiting, astride a lean-flanked gray mare. "I am going to ride along beside you," he said defiantly.

"Tom," said Aunt Maria, her voice ominous, "you would cause an accident if you did so—you know Daisy does not like other horses near her."

The pony hitched to the trap stamped her feet, as if concurring, and tossed her head, snorting, as Tom's mare shifted a little. Tom shot his mother an angry glance, then wheeled, and put his mare at a gallop. They watched the dust fly up behind him as he vanished down the drive. Tom had an excellent seat on a horse, she saw, and a little spurt of liking for him grew inside her. Sabrina had great respect for physical courage.

When Aunt Maria was seated in the trap, there was little room for a second, let alone a third, but dutifully the two girls squeezed themselves into the tiny space left and, with polite smiles, assured their aunt that they were comfortable.

"I knew there would be room," she said with satisfaction.

They set off at a labored trot down the drive. Their weight made the trap a little unsteady, and their pace was hardly spectacular, but when they turned into the lane leading down hill to Ambresbury, they began to move faster. The weight of the trap gave impetus to the descent, and Sabrina began to feel quite nervous as she saw the green banks flying past.

The wheels rattled loudly. Earth and stones flew up, spattering their clothes. One hit Aunt Maria on the eye and she relaxed her grip on the reins for a moment to rub the wounded part, only to find the pony, frightened by the clattering of the trap behind her, bolting away, completely out of control.

"We shall overturn on the bend," Aunt Maria cried in alarm, abandoning her dignity. "I cannot hold her . . ."

"Give me the reins, Aunt," Sabrina ordered, throwing herself forward and seizing the reins from her aunt's limp hands.

"We shall all be killed," moaned Aunt Maria.

Charity shrank into herself, her hands clenched, but was silent, watching her sister intently.

"There is a stone bridge at the corner," Aunt Maria shrieked, "if we hit it, we shall be killed . . ."

Sabrina pulled on the reins until she was certain that her arms must be dislocated at the shoulder, but the pony galloped on without a pause.

"It is the weight of the trap," she shouted, "we are too heavy for her."

The dangerous corner was approaching fast. Sabrina's mind worked furiously. Should they attempt to jump out? She felt she might do so, but not Charity, or Aunt Maria. Their nerves would not be equal to the task.

Suddenly her eye caught a gate on the right, leading into a field. A boy in a smock was opening it. Towards the gate streamed a line of sheep, a dog at their heels, crawling along, his eyes sharply aware of each movement in the flock.

"Back! Get back!" shouted Sabrina, making violent motions of the arm towards the boy.

He stood, staring, his mouth open.

"I am coming through there!" she shouted, pulling hard on the reins.

The pony swerved violently to the right in response, and then, seizing this chance of escape, scraped through the gate with a splintering of wood. The boy tumbled backwards in alarm among his sheep.

The trap bumped up into the air and then turned over on its side and fell. Aunt Maria, Charity and Sabrina were hurled out, but thrown clear of the trap, landing on muddy grass in a heap of blown skirts, struggling limbs and crushed bonnets.

Sabrina wriggled up from under Charity's weight, sat upright, and gave Aunt Maria, who was groaning, a tug. The blue bonnet came up, dented and muddy, and under it was Aunt Maria's white face, streaked with grass and bleeding slightly from a scratch down the very center of her nose.

"My legs," she moaned, clutching at them.

"Do they hurt?" Sabrina knelt and gently felt them. "Tell me where they hurt? They do not seem to be broken."

"I ache from head to foot," said Aunt Maria, as Sabrina helped her to her feet. "That silly, useless trap!" She turned on the boy who was staring at her in wonderment. "Why are you gaping at us, you great gooby?"

Quietly Sabrina said, "Will you help me cut the tackle and set the pony free before it kills itself?"

The lad shuffled forward, and together they freed the wildly kicking pony. With rolling eyes and sweating coat, it plunged away, baring its teeth in terror, obviously beside itself.

"We must leave her in the field. She is in no condition to be touched," said Sabrina.

"We will have to walk back to the house, then," said Aunt Maria irritably, "uphill all the way!"

"If you are too tired, Aunt, I could go and send help back," offered Sabrina.

Aunt Maria shook her head, "Sit here, on this damp grass? No, I thank you. It would be more comfortable to walk."

"Then take my arm," Sabrina said, and turned to

smile at Charity, "and you take the other arm! We will help each other."

They set off at a steady pace, but Sabrina slowly noticed that Charity was limping and paused. "You have hurt your ankle?" she asked. "Is it very painful?"

"I can manage," Charity said, smiling, but her cheeks were very pale, and Sabrina saw that she was trembling a little.

"Let me see," she ordered, crouching to unbutton her sister's boots.

It was immediately clear that the ankle was very swollen and painful. When Sabrina touched the dark swelling, Charity winced.

"You cannot walk on that," Sabrina said fiercely, looking round in despair for some sign of another human being who might help.

"If only I had not sent Tom away," groaned Aunt Maria.

Sabrina spared no ironic glance, but she had to echo the sentiment.

"Listen," said Charity, "is that a horse trotting?"

They stood, listening, and soon were convinced that the sound was the tip-tap of hooves coming up the lane from the village.

"It must be Tom," cried Aunt Maria in relief.

They faced down the hill, waiting, and then, as the horseman came into view, Sabrina's heart gave a great thud of fear and distress, and her skin grew cold as ice. It was not Tom. She knew at a glance who it was, and when Aunt Maria confirmed her fears, she bit her lip to silence a cry of protest.

"Why, it is Dr. Graham," Aunt Maria said warmly, "the very man we need!"

Sabrina drew herself up in readiness. The moment had come upon her when she least expected it, had least resistance to the pain of the meeting. The late shock to her nerves had left her weakened. She had to steel herself for this encounter with the last of her small resources of pride and courage.

Too soon he was level with them, his horse reined in, lifting his hat and greeting Aunt Maria with cool courtesy. Then his glance skimmed to the two girls, with idle curiosity, and Sabrina saw the shocked amazement in his face as their eyes met. His eyes widened, his face lost all its healthy color. He stared, stiffening in his seat. Then he seemed to pull himself together, with a clear physical effort, and turned back to Aunt Maria who was already pouring out her story and bemoaning Charity's injury and her own feeling of weakness.

Sabrina allowed herself to watch him, assuring herself that the three years since their last meeting gave her reason enough to be curious as to any changes in his appearance. There appeared to her to be none. His hair still sprang black and curly from his head, his eyes were still a very dark blue, his features regular and handsome.

If there was a change, it was in his manner. She had known him as a gay, lively companion, full of fun, impudently teasing, warm and confiding. He seemed older than the passage of three years would warrant. His tone was courteously grave as he spoke to her aunt. She sensed a reserve, a quietness which had not been apparent before. He had adopted the famous bedside manner which had made his uncle famous in London society.

"So clever of Sabrina to turn the animal off the road," Aunt Maria was saying, "I am convinced we would have broken our necks on the stone bridge at the corner."

Sabrina saw him half turn his head towards her, almost involuntarily. "Very intelligent of her," he said softly.

"But you have not met my nieces," said Aunt Maria. "This is Sabrina, the eldest, and this is Charity. Girls, this is our good Doctor Graham who has been so kind to poor little Victoria." To Aunt Maria, a kindness to her children was a passport to her good books in anyone, particularly when that person was a handsome young man with good prospects in the world.

Sabrina curtsied, her eyes lowered. She knew when his glance touched her once more and flicked away rapidly to her sister.

"I suggest our best plan is for me to take Miss Charity up on my horse," he said, "the sooner she is home, the better. Then I can take a look at this swollen ankle."

"So kind," murmured Aunt Maria.

He dismounted, lifted Charity gently to his saddle in one swift movement, and in a moment, they were all walking up the hill, with Johnny leading his mount and Charity, side saddle, biting her lip nervously as the horse jogged along. She had never ridden before and was very frightened of horses, but not for worlds would she have betrayed her fear.

Sabrina, reading her expression rightly, smiled comfortingly at her.

Aunt Maria walked beside him, chattering about local affairs. Sabrina walked behind, watching the set of his broad shoulders, the turn of his head, listening intently for his quiet voice as he responded briefly, from time to time.

If only, she thought, I knew his intentions. Oh, for the gift of mind-reading for just this moment. What is going on inside his head? What does he mean to do about me? Will he tell my uncle and aunt about my dismissal from his uncle's house and the reason for it?

It was impossible to tell, by his manner, what he was thinking. He had learned to wear a mask. His handsome face was as calm and unresponsive as a sheet of white paper.

Tom galloped up just as they reached the drive and looked amazed to see them walking. His mother poured out the story, expressing regret that he had not been with them.

"Well, that was your doing, you know, Mama," he said, grinning over her head at Sabrina, "I would have been very happy to escort you, but you would have none of it."

She did not answer.

"You look quite done up, cousin Sabrina," Tom went on, "let me take you up to the house."

"Of course, I am not tired," said his mother, in a complaining tone, "I am as strong as an ox and need expect no sympathy from ungrateful children."

"You will never go near a horse if you can avoid

it, Mama," he retorted. "I did not think you would wish to ride."

"You did not ask me," she said.

"I am quite able to walk the rest of the way, thank you, Tom," Sabrina said quickly, to avoid further argument, seeing that Tom was determined to be difficult.

He shrugged. "Well, then, up you get, Mama," he said, and took her by the waist and tried to hoist her into the saddle. She cried out crossly that he was hurting her, and Johnny quietly left his own horse for a moment to assist her.

"Thank you, Dr. Graham," she panted, holding nervously to the long gray mane of the horse.

"Do not clutch at the mane like that," Tom said. "You look like someone sitting on a keg of gunpowder. You are quite safe you know."

"I do not feel it," she whined.

"I told you that you would hate riding the horse, but you are such a dog in the manger, you would do it. So do not complain to me if you are uncomfortable." And Tom led her away, crossly criticizing her behavior as he went.

Johnny shot Sabrina a long, hard glance, before turning back to Charity, and she felt the hot color rush into her face.

At last they were inside the house, and Charity was carried up to her room.

Johnny gently examined her. "It is nothing serious," he told them, drying his hands afterwards. "The ankle is swollen, but there is no other injury. That wet poultice should soothe it, and a rest will do the work in a day or two. I want you to stay in bed until Sunday." And he smiled at Charity.

She looked distressed. "My aunt . . ."

"Will be grateful it is no worse, I am sure," he said. He walked to the door. "A word with you, Miss Crammond," he said to Sabrina, without looking at her, then to Charity, "Good day, Miss Charity!"

Charity looked enquiringly at Sabrina,. who shrugged as if puzzled, before following him out of the room.

He was on the landing, leaning against the wall in an attitude of indolence. She stood in front of him, eyes lowered, waiting for the blow to fall.

"You took your time," he drawled. "We cannot talk here, can we? Walls have ears. I will meet you in the shrubberies in fifteen minutes. I have to see Victoria, and then I will walk round the back of the house to the stables. Wait for me there." He turned and went up the next flight of stairs without a glance, and she stood frozen, shivering, wrapping her arms around herself.

Then, with an effort, she roused herself and went downstairs and out into the garden.

It was twenty minutes before he came out. She had been walking to and fro, watching the black-birds searching for grubs under the laurel bushes, feeling the cold spring sunshine on her face and the fresh tang of the wind in her nostrils, but her whole mind concentrated on the house, watching for him.

Yet when he came at last, she was not watching because she had found the white wing feather of a dove lying under a bush and had idly begun to scratch on a laurel leaf with the tip.

"Writing your true love's name?" he asked with soft irony.

She started, and the feather floated out of her hand. They both stood, watching it fall, as if it were important.

Then she looked up at him, defiantly meeting his eyes. "Well?" she asked, determined to face it out. She had decided in the waiting period that she would neither explain nor argue. He had believed her guilty without even asking for her version of events, and she would not stoop to justify herself to him. He was not worth such an effort. Let him believe what he chose.

"Do your family know what happened in London?" he asked. "Did you tell them the truth, or make up some cock-and-bull story to satisfy them?"

She flushed angrily. "They do not even know I ever held a position, I imagine. My sister has never asked me anything, and she is the only one who knows."

"Your sister?" He stared at her, his face thoughtful. "Yes, I had forgotten her. So your uncle knows nothing?"

"Nothing."

"I have just been speaking to your aunt," he said, after a moment. "She has confided in me her doubts about having you in the house . . ."

"Indeed?" she echoed, stiffening with fury. How could Aunt Maria discuss such a matter, she wondered? And with him, of all people!

His lip curled sardonically. "She is anxious, it appears, because young Tom shows signs of being attracted to you. I imagine you know what manner of fool he made of himself at Oxford, getting involved with some girl. Your uncle had to buy the girl's father off, and they do not wish to have another such incident."

"They need not worry," she said scornfully.

"Oh, but they do," he said mockingly. "You would be more expensive, no doubt. And Tom is on the point of becoming betrothed to a very sweet girl. This is the worst possible moment for him to kick over the traces again."

"And so you told her how I was dismissed from your uncle's house, I suppose?"

His face hardened. "No, I am almost as big a fool as Tom. I did not." Then, seeing her eyes widen and lift to his, "Oh, I meant to do so—but I thought I might attain the same result without telling tales. If you know I have it in my power to tell them, it may make you more careful. So, remember, keep Tom at a distance, or your aunt shall hear the whole story."

"You do not know the whole story," she cried in angry humiliation. "You have never asked me what happened . . ."

"I trust my own eyes more than I trust your tongue," he drawled scornfully. "I saw you, remember. Fortunately! I might have been duped had I only heard the tale at secondhand. I was too besotted with you at the time. Any lie you spun for me would have fooled me. But I saw you in his arms . . ." And his face glared at her, harsh with repudiation.

She opened her mouth to protest, but pride choked her voice, and she closed it again, swallowing the bile of humiliation and misery. She turned to walk away, but he caught her by the shoulder and, taken off balance, she stumbled and fell against him. For a second their bodies touched, and she felt a violent jerk on every nerve, as though she had been struck by lightning.

"Do not forget," he said, thickly, "you are walking a tightrope. Keep away from Tom." And then she heard the laurels rustle as he walked away, heard the crunch of his feet on the gravel path. She was momentarily blind, trembling from the shock. Then she, too, went back to the house and up to her room, where she sat forcing herself back to some semblance of normality before going to see Charity.

Even so, when Charity saw her, she was immediately aware of some change in her. She stared at her, and asked, "Are you ill, Sabrina? You are very pale."

Sabrina made some feeble excuse and managed to change the subject, but Charity watched her from time to time with uneasy eyes.

Johnny came to the house daily for the next week. "I have two very pretty patients here at Ambreys," he told Aunt Maria charmingly. "My other patients will begin to complain, I spend so much time here, but it is hard not to be tempted. There are so many delightful young ladies at Ambreys now." And his glance, lightly, mockingly, flickered over Sabrina and returned to her aunt almost before either of them was aware of any change in his expression.

Conscious of suffocating anger, Sabrina bent over her sewing, ignoring him. How dare he taunt her in that fashion?

Louisa came into the room to bring Sabrina another of her petticoats. Sabrina had offered to sew new lace on them, and Louisa, seeing the delicacy of Sabrina's needlework, had accepted eagerly. Now, when she entered, a little flush crept into her sallow cheeks as she responded to Johnny's bow, and Sabrina, catching the complacent smile of her aunt, suddenly guessed at another of her aunt's matchmaking plans. Was he aware of it, though, she pondered, and, seeing his attentive attitude, suspected that he was prepared to be compliant.

"I hope you will delight us with one of your songs at this dinner party, Miss Louisa?" he asked.

She nervously smiled.

"I . . ." she stammered, "I am . . ."

"She is always so shy," her mother interrupted, coming to the rescue, "but people are always so kind about her voice. She is a silly girl to be nervous of public performance."

"You have a very pretty voice, Miss Louisa," he agreed. "I must insist that you sing for us."

Louisa looked down and plaited her fingers. "You are very kind, sir."

The door opened, and the butler trod in deferentially. "Mr. Johnstone, Madam," he murmured, standing back to admit a tall gentleman in riding clothes.

Aunt Maria smiled, holding out her hand. "My dear, dear sir, how very kind of you."

The newcomer crossed to touch her hand. He was a thin, weather-beaten man of thirty or so, Sabrina guessed, with shrewd gray eyes and a friendly, easy manner. His fair hair was very fine and short, brushed back to give his face added length, which emphasized the narrow features and long, aquiline nose.

"I brought some fruit and a parcel of children's

books for Miss Victoria," he said. "She must be lonely up in the nursery all day."

"How thoughtful. She will be so grateful. Thank you very much." Aunt Maria beamed upon him. "I am afraid she is rather cross and fretful at the moment."

"Ah, getting better, then?" he said, smiling, turning to Johnny with a nod of recognition. "I fancy that is the reason, eh, Doctor?"

Johnny agreed. "Convalescence is always painful for children. Once they begin to get better, they wish to be out of doors."

"Just so," said Mr. Johnstone, turning to smile at Louisa, "Good morning, Miss Louisa." Then his glance switched to Sabrina, and his eyes widened in interest and admiration.

Aunt Maria said, "This is my elder niece, Sabrina Crammond. Sabrina, my dear, this is Mr. Johnstone of High Lodge. Mr. Johnstone has one of the most efficient farms in the country. Very modern and the envy of all our other local farmers."

"They do not have the necessary capital," he said quickly. "That is the answer to farming today. Capital! Too many farmers live from hand to mouth. Each year is a gamble for them. Whereas I can afford to be patient and wait for nature to be kind." He came to take Sabrina's hand, raising it to his lips in an oddly foreign gesture. "I am very happy to meet you, Miss Crammond. I am sure you are not interested in farming . . ."

"Oh, but I am," she said quickly. "I am interested in everything. My Papa always used to say that one cannot afford to ignore any detail of life."

His gray eyes smiled at her. "Your Papa was a clever man, then. And if you are serious about the farm, I hope you will allow me to show you round it one day." He smiled at Louisa. "Perhaps all you young ladies would care to visit me. I have been meaning to have a picnic party in the summer. There is a charming spot by the river which is ideal for a picnic."

Aunt Maria answered for her daughter, "Oh, delightful! We will be very happy to come, I am sure. Will we not, Louisa?"

Louisa murmured something inaudibly, gazing at the carpet with a very flushed face.

Sabrina glanced up and met Johnny's cool, hard gaze. His eyes bit deep into hers as if questioning her, then he looked away with a slight shrug.

Mr. Johnstone took a seat beside her and began to ask her about her impressions of the neighborhood, and then to talk of Cambridge, which he had visited from time to time. "My father was a corn merchant in Colchester," he told her. "He intended me to take over the business, but I had a bent for farming, and when he died, I sold up and bought my farm. I would have liked to have some time at the university, but corn merchants do not need more than a smattering of education, or so my father thought." He smiled at her. "I regret that. I found Cambridge a fascinating place."

"Yes, it is," she agreed. "There is an air of tranquillity about it, at least in the vacations. During the term it is a little wearing on the nerves. The young men can be noisy."

"I am sure they flocked to your father's house," he said with an amused smile. "Such an attraction must have acted like a magnet!"

She laughed, glancing down.

"Do you hunt, Miss Crammond?" he asked, after a brief pause.

She shook her head.

"But you ride?"

"I have had little opportunity," she said.

"If that is true, then I can only say that it is a pity," he said. "I am convinced you must be a born huntswoman."

"Oh, absolutely," drawled Johnny, meeting Sabrina's startled glance with an ironic smile, "a born huntswoman, Johnstone."

She caught the double meaning in his words and flushed. Was she to be perpetually reminded of the past? It was like living with a sword suspended over her head. She faced him, her eyes hot and angry, words of protest burning her lips, but unsaid.

Mr. Johnstone looked from one to the other of them, his brows raised curiously.

Aunt Maria, unknowingly, saved the situation. "Louisa would love to hunt," she said crossly, "if it were not for her bad health and delicate nerves. I do not believe a young lady should enjoy hunting. It is a pursuit for the gentlemen and must be an affront to the sensibilities of a young lady."

Mr. Johnstone protested, but politely. "It is true, some young ladies are too delicate for hunting, but I think it is not a general rule."

Aunt Maria, having forced herself and Louisa

back into the conversation, began to talk of her coming dinner party to which Mr. Johnstone was invited, and Sabrina could sink back into quiet isolation, her head bent over her sewing.

When Mr. Johnstone left, he smiled down at her warmly, "A great pleasure to have met you, Miss Crammond. I look forward to our next meeting with pleasant anticipation."

Conscious of Johnny's attentive ears, she murmured a polite reply.

Then Johnny paused, waiting for a moment to allow her aunt and cousin to walk ahead with Mr. Johnstone, before saying, "You waste no time in transferring your lure to another victim. Congratulations. I would say a hit, a palpable hit!"

She met his mocking gaze with a defiant look. "My cousin was the forbidden object, I believe," she said steadily.

"Oh, indeed. I can have no objections to seeing Johnstone caught in your net." He paused, glancing away. "No objections," he repeated in an odd voice.

"Must you continuously torment me, then?" she asked in a low voice. "Why make remarks which bring us both to the edge of arousing the curiosity of others? Mr. Johnstone noticed the way you spoke to me. He looked very oddly at us."

"Mea culpa," he said softly. "I fell into temptation. I will try to curb my tongue in the future. Of course, the poor fellow must discover for himself what I so providentially found out before it was too late." And his dark blue eyes flashed down at her, suddenly stormy with anger. "That you are a . . ."

he stopped, biting his lip. "No," he said, "not in a drawing room. Let us draw a veil over what you are; let us be polite and distant. Good afternoon, Miss Crammond. Your servant, Miss Crammond." And he bowed, a bright, hard smile on his face, and left her.

CHAPTER THREE

When Charity was allowed to come downstairs, at last, and sit in the morning room, reading or sewing as the fancy took her, she found her sister completely absorbed in domestic duties for their aunt and was forced to fall back upon the company of her cousin, Louisa.

Louisa, freed from her mother's dominating presence, slowly thawed out. For the first time in her life, she had found someone shyer than herself who would listen, respond and even admire. The experience excited her. Accustomed to her mother's smothering affection, her brother's easy scorn, she had withdrawn into a citadel of discontent from which she had glowered at the world. Charity's gentle sympathy lured her out, and in her presence the sullen look evaporated. Louisa even laughed or looked animated from time to time.

Charity's deft fingers were put to work to find a new hair style for Louisa. "You need to give the illusion of height," she murmured, piling the hair up, and standing back to view the effect.

Aunt Maria bustled in, stopped, stared, and said, "Gracious heavens, Louisa, what have you done to your hair?"

The sullen look came back; Louisa's lip drooped.

"It is pretty, is it not, Aunt?" Charity said eagerly. "I think it gives Louisa more height and more assurance . . ."

Aunt Maria walked round, eyeing her daughter with growing complacency. "Well, well, it is plain you have been amusing yourselves to some effect. Very pretty, indeed. You must arrange Louisa's hair for her on the day of our dinner party, Charity."

Breathlessly Louisa asked, "May I keep it like this, Mama?"

"It looks very well. Yes, you may keep it so. It will give an air of real elegance to your new gown."

And Dr. Graham, arriving to visit Victoria, said, "There is to be some breaking of hearts, I see, ma'am. Your daughter and her cousin are dangerous young women, plotting the downfall of our eligible bachelors in their secret councils of war. I shall have to warn the neighborhood."

Unaccustomed to such teasing, Louisa flushed dark red, her lower lip trembling, and stared at her feet.

"You must save the place beside your daughter for me, ma'am," Dr. Graham continued. "I will put my heart in jeopardy for the sake of my fellows."

Aunt Maria laughed coyly. "You are making the child blush, Doctor. You must not tease her so." But her smile was indulgent, and her eyes encouraged him.

Since both Charity and Sabrina were in enforced mourning, they had no real choice in what they wore for the dinner party. Their aunt inspected their wardrobes with sighs and shakings of the head, and allowed that their simple black gowns would do for the occasion.

"And no jewelry, of course," she said, satisfaction in her eyes but regret in her voice. Their subdued attire would not cast either Louisa or Charlotte Colling into the shade.

The family at Ambreys had gone into mourning for James Crammond for a month, but the month was now up, and they were slowly moving into white, purple and lavender, the acceptable semi-mourning. Mourning for the daughters of the deceased, however, must continue for six months, and Aunt Maria, surveying the two girls in their somber gowns, was enchanted that it should be so, yet careful to maintain a pretense of regret.

She was not an unkindly woman. Had she had no children, or were her children all gone out into the world, she would have been prepared to show great kindness to the two orphaned nieces of her husband. But with two daughters to provide for and a son to protect, she was made uneasy by Sabrina's beauty and spirit. Into the nest of a hedge sparrow had flown a jay of startling coloring, and the situation demanded ruthless tactics.

Sabrina, studying herself in the mirror on the evening of the dinner party, was pleased to be reminded that black suited her. Against the dull sheen of the material, her red hair blazed, falling in deliberately disheveled ringlets around her face, her creamy skin glowing, pearly and smooth. Her lack of ornament was no drawback. With her hair and features, she needed no jewelry.

She walked into her sister's bedroom and found

Louisa, seated on the bed, watching Pearton put the finishing touches to Charity's toilette. Charity, as always, was insignificant in her black gown, her face pale, her golden ringlets falling over her bare shoulders in limp strands.

Charity had dressed Louisa's hair herself and drew Sabrina's attention to it with pride. She had drawn some of the hair up on top of the head and added false ringlets to cover the deficiency at the sides. Louisa looked taller, slimmer, more elegant, and her color testified to her own newfound confidence.

She got up, her skirts billowing, and complained of the tightness of her bodice and the fullness of her skirts.

"You have to suffer to be beautiful," Sabrina quoted dryly, having heard Aunt Maria make this remark so often, and the three girls laughed.

They walked down together. Sabrina saw that Charity shivered nervously as they reached the hall and put an arm around her.

"Goose," she teased, to coax a smile again, "it is a dinner party, not an execution!"

Charity smiled dutifully, but remained pale. Above the black gown, her face seemed disembodied, a white wraith of a face floating between the delicate ringlets, her blue eyes staring out in agonized anxiety.

Aunt Maria greeted them with an excess of nervousness, "Oh, Louisa, you look very well. Have you seen to the wine, Sabrina? They never have it just right, and Sir George Colling is quite a good judge of wine. Louisa, dear, try to stand straight. If you stoop, it will make you look quite round-shouldered. The table, Sabrina, have you checked the table?"

"I did so before I went up to dress," Sabrina soothed. "It looks very fine."

"The silver? There are no finger marks on the silver? Those girls will leave finger marks. Oh, Sabrina, the flowers . . ."

"All is as it should be," Sabrina said patiently. "You remember, I arranged the flowers myself. Spring flowers and feathery grass. They look extremely pretty, especially the daffodils."

Gratefully, Aunt Maria said, "You have been so good, Sabrina. I do not know what I should have done without you." Her restless eye fell again upon Louisa standing stolidly nearby, her over-elaborate dress, lavender ruched with white and heavily trimmed with lace upon the tight-fitting sleeves, giving her an air of comic rotundity which even her new hair style could not quite offset. "Oh, Louisa, do try to stand more elegantly. You look so . . ." Words failed her, and she groaned, and turning to Sabrina said, "I wish that you could teach her to walk gracefully. She walks as if her limbs were carved from wood."

The men came in. Uncle Matthew was uneasy in his formal evening attire; Tom in his long tailcoat and pantaloons, was gay, excited and in festive mood. He threw his mother a bow, his sister a careless, "You look like a cake in that gown, Louisa," and turned to Sabrina with a quick, skimming glance of admiration. "You should never wear anything but black, cousin. It suits you to perfection."

Aunt Maria, staring, bit her lip. But before she could speak, the guests began to arrive, and she and her husband went out into the hall to welcome them.

As the house filled with people, a new atmosphere became apparent. Silently, softly, the servants passed around, weaving between the gossiping guests with trays of sherry. Flushed and nervous, Aunt Maria fluttered round the room, her full skirts bouncing, speaking to the little groups, watching the servants, eyeing Louisa with mingled indulgence and anxiety.

Byrd Johnstone stood with Sabrina and Louisa, talking of hunting, his weather-beaten appearance made quite distinguished by the formality of his evening dress. Louisa was bored by talk of horses and fell to fiddling with her sleeves, pulling at the lace nervously with an air of inattention.

Sabrina, enjoying Mr. Johnstone's very sensible conversation, threw her cousin a warning glance under cover of her fan, having caught sight of Aunt Maria's ominous watchfulness from across the room.

Smoothing back his flat fair hair, Mr. Johnstone observed that the weather seemed to have set fine. "Perhaps we shall be able to have that picnic soon, Miss Crammond. I hope you mean to keep your promise and come to view my farm."

"I should like it very much," she assured him.

"I know you young ladies are fond of young animals," he said, smiling, "and springtime is the very season, you know, for things of that sort. The lambs will be past being interesting if you delay beyond May. We must set a date soon."

Louisa, brought to awareness of her mother's stern gaze, burst out with strange enthusiasm, "Oh, delightful! I shall so look forward to it!" And, finding herself surveyed by both her cousin and the gentlemen with surprise, blushed violently and once more retreated behind a wall of silence.

Sabrina, pitying her, yet amused despite herself, looked down, compressing her lips to suppress a smile, and, on looking up, found Mr. Johnstone watching her with such a light of humor in his eyes that the smile would come out, and did, with a quick response from him.

And, at that moment, Sabrina heard Johnny's voice behind her, raised in apology for his late arrival. A flush burned its way into her cheeks. She saw Mr. Johnstone's eye notice her change of color, and his fine eyebrows rise in inquiry.

Relieved that all her guests were now arrived, Aunt Maria nodded to the butler, and the gong soon summoned them through to the dining room.

Sabrina found herself being taken into dinner by Mr. Johnstone who murmured into her ear that he was very happy to be sitting next to her. He had heard of her escapade with the runaway pony and was full of admiration.

"Girls are not usually so quick-witted," he said. "I can think of none among my acquaintance, except perhaps Miss Colling, who is a famous horsewoman and shows us all the way in the field."

"Really?" Sabrina asked, glancing over the table at Miss Colling with interest.

Charlotte Colling had no pretense of beauty, and the heavy yellow silk she wore, encrusted with fine lace, gave to her sallow complexion a pronounced air of jaundice. Her heavy brown hair was dressed in the fashionable ringlets, cascading down into the tight bodice of her dress. Her face was long, broad and equine. Her eyes a warm brown, her teeth very good, but large enough to make her likeness to a horse more than evident.

Meeting Sabrina's glance, she smiled, and with that smile, brought a warmth into Sabrina's face, for her glance was direct and frank, her smile endearing.

"Do you hunt, Miss Crammond?" she asked, and upon Sabrina's explanation that she had never been into the field, joined Mr. Johnstone in declaring that she must do so, and as soon as possible.

"I will introduce you to the hunt, Sabrina," Tom interrupted, leaning forward eagerly from his seat beside Charlotte.

"I have already claimed that honor," Byrd Johnstone said with a smile.

"She's my cousin, damn you," Tom growled.

There was a hush around the table, and Aunt Maria stiffened, throwing Sabrina a look of furious reproach.

Then Johnny said, his lip curling, "I should say the honor goes to Mr. Wilton," and, turning to Uncle Matthew, "Eh, sir?"

Purple, his eyes sharp, Uncle Matthew said loudly, "Yes, it is certainly my responsibility, and I shall see to it that Sabrina has a mount suitable to her."

Carefully avoiding Johnny's eye, Sabrina shot a glance at Charlotte, and was dismayed to see her staring at her plate with a heavy flush, her lip between her teeth.

The hum of noise around the table began once more, a little louder, as if each one tried to drown the recent little episode with frothy chatter.

Sir George Colling divided his time between Aunt

Maria, beside whom he sat, and his wife, talking indifferently to both at rare intervals. He was a stout, red-faced man with a great appetite, and his dinner engrossed all his real attention. His wife gave Sabrina a number of hard, unfriendly looks, picking at her meal as if each mouthful choked her. A long, horse-faced woman, it was clear where Charlotte's features came from. She wore a plum-colored gown which revealed the bony cavities of neck and shoulders, and a brilliant, over-elaborate necklace which threw off light as she moved.

"Do you not miss your Cambridge friends?" Mr. Johnstone asked Sabrina.

"We had very few," she replied honestly. "My Papa was not a social man."

He gave her a quick, shrewd glance. "Then this is quite a change for you? I congratulate you. Nobody would guess from your manner that you were unaccustomed to social gatherings of this size."

She smiled, thanking him and, as she looked up, met Johnny's dark blue gaze. Their eyes collided, froze, moved on quickly, as if both were nervous.

After dinner, while the gentlemen remained behind to circulate the port and nuts, the ladies withdrew to talk of children, bonnets, husbands, with polite indifference.

Aunt Maria sat with Lady Colling on the chaise longue, their heads together as they discussed the betrothal of their children. Once or twice Sabrina felt their eyes upon her back and knew herself the topic of discussion.

She sat with Charity and Louisa on another of the velvet-covered sofas, with Charlotte Colling insisting on taking a seat on a little footstool near the fire from where she could join their conversation and toast her hands at the same time.

Seeing Sabrina's glance resting on her yellow gown, she laughed and said directly, "I know I look a fright in it, but Mama would have it! And, quite frankly, I look a fright in everything but my riding habit."

"Simple, well-cut clothes are always the most becoming, aren't they?" said Sabrina, returning the smile. "I have the same problem. Pretty clothes make me look ridiculous. Lace and frills are all very well on someone like my sister, who is small and delicate, but we are not all built the same."

Charlotte gave her a startled look. "You look very handsome indeed in that gown, Miss Crammond."

"It is very simple," Sabrina pointed out. "You should see me in pink! I look like a boiled shrimp."

The girls all burst out into giggles and drew the half indulgent glance of their elders upon them.

In an excess of enjoyment, Charlotte said warmly, "I do hope I shall see you out with the hunt this year. I am the only female in the district who can tackle anything higher than a lavender bush. They are a weak-spirited lot of girls." Then, catching Louisa's eye, "Oh, not you, of course, Louisa."

Drawn out by this frank exchange of views, Louisa said firmly, "Yes, I am. I am terrified of horses. I hate hunting. I am on the side of the fox. I think it a great shame to hunt such a pretty creature."

Charity chimed in, "So do I!" And they surveyed each other with satisfaction of mutual agreement.

"We cannot have this, can we, Sabrina?" Charlotte

said, grinning at her. "Do say you will come out and show them the way. I wish I had seen you take that runaway pony off the road into the field. Just the most sporting thing I have ever heard of!"

"If I am still here in the autumn, I shall be very pleased to do so," Sabrina said.

The men joined them shortly, and the room began to be crowded once more, with the groups of women breaking up as they were attracted away by more interesting company. There were several married couples among the guests, who gravitated to each other, absorbed in discussions of children and domestic details, but the younger guests tended to congregate at one end of the room in a large group.

Tom came, like a flame-drawn moth, towards the girls, and Sabrina saw Charlotte's brown eyes turn hopefully towards him. Poor Charlotte, she thought, recognizing the look of love, and herself turned away, hoping to elude Tom's eager glance.

She found herself brushing against Johnny, lean and elegant in his evening clothes, his dark blue eyes flickering over her with hurtful indifference.

"Enjoying yourself?" he murmured, his lip curling up, and she pretended not to hear.

"Miss Crammond, do come and sit beside me and tell me more about Cambridge," said Byrd Johnstone's level voice at her elbow.

Gratefully, she let him lead her to a seat and sank down with a froth of skirts. He leaned beside her chair, smiling down.

"Tell me about yourself," he ordered. "What are your favorite pursuits? Painting, sewing, playing the piano?"

"I enjoy playing the piano," she admitted.

"Then you must play for us later," he said, and they went on to talk of music for some time.

Once, she heard Johnny laughing a few feet away, and involuntarily turned to look at him. He was leaning over Louisa's chair, his head bent, but, as if he felt her gaze, he looked up. Mockery flickered over her from those blue eyes, then he looked away. She felt herself flushing and stiffened against a sting of pain.

Byrd Johnstone had stopped, mid-sentence, and when she looked up, she found him watching her, his narrow face intent.

"Have you known Graham long?" he asked suddenly, and the question caught her off balance.

Stammering, pink to the ears, she answered untruthfully, "No, not very long." And, changing the subject, "Do you know the old British camp in the forest, Mr. Johnstone?"

"Ambresbury Banks?" he asked, his eyes shrewdly watching her face. "Yes, I have visited it once or twice. Are you interested at all in antiquities, Miss Crammond?"

"My Papa was very careful to give us a good classical education," she said, "and he spoke to us once of Ambresbury Banks. Is it an interesting site?"

"That you must judge for yourself," he said. "We will have to arrange a carriage outing there one summer day. It is too wet underfoot at present."

It was late when the guests departed. Aunt Maria stood in the hall, yawning as she said goodnight to her family. Embracing Tom, who submitted ungraciously, she said, "My dear, dear boy! It is all decided. Your father is to instruct his lawyer to draw up the marriage settlements tomorrow, and the betrothal is to be announced on Charlotte's birthday. There is to be a ball at the Grange; no expense to be spared, everyone in the neighborhood to be invited, champagne, an orchestra! It will be the talk of the district!" Flushed and excited, she gazed around her. "Oh, I shall never sleep tonight!" And, yawning, she departed for her bed.

At breakfast next morning, Uncle Matthew was weary, red-eyed and irritable. "I must be doing something about the schoolmistress," he said, picking at his bloater with distaste. "I will drive over to Epping and call on Devenish to instruct him in this business of the marriage settlements. He may have heard of somebody suitable for the new school by now. I asked him to keep his ears open."

"There must be someone who would do," said Aunt Maria, "and I do believe I will accompany you, Matthew. I have shopping to do, and I feel in the need for some fresh air after all my exertions about the dinner party."

Uncle Matthew nodded without enthusiasm. "We might eat our luncheon at the Cock," he offered, "unless Devenish asks us to luncheon."

"Oh, I would much prefer the Cock," said Aunt Maria. "Mrs. Devenish is quite the most ingratiating female I have ever met. She might wish us to return the invitation."

"I have had luncheon there before now," said her husband sturdily.

"Yes, my love, but that is quite a different matter.

There, you are a business client. If I am with you, however, no such thing! No, much better not."

"As you please," he growled, rising.

Charity and Louisa disappeared upstairs to giggle in their bedroom over some novels which had arrived from London, and Sabrina, without occupation in her aunt's absence, wandered into the garden.

It was April, and the sun was just beginning to acquire a cool warmth. Daffodils, tulips and crocuses were filling the garden borders with color, and the leaves were breaking out of bud on the trees. A sweet, fresh scent blew in the wind. It had rained during the night. The flowers breathed a delicate perfume, and the earth was black and moist.

She turned into the shrubberies to protect her shoes from the damp grass and walked slowly round the twisting gravel paths, flicking a raindrop off a matt green leaf, startling a starling which was grubbing under the bushes.

She had enough to occupy her thoughts for the time to pass rapidly. She had slept badly the night before, her dreams broken with threatening images of Johnny, recurring nightmares of exposure and dismissal from Ambreys. Charity's deepening friendship with Louisa was a comfort to her. She could feel that her sister was slowly growing happy here, relaxing the stern guard she had learned to impose upon herself. Listening to the two younger girls giggling together, she had for the first time seen Charity as she ought to be, young, carefree, at ease. She was terrified that that newfound happiness might be blasted by Johnny's revelations. For herself, to leave Ambreys would be hard, for she had learned to love the house, but her real fear was for Charity. Ambreys, for her sister, was sanctuary. She must not be forced out of it.

She was so engrossed in her thoughts that she did not see Tom come out of the house and stealthily approach her.

Half turning to watch a pigeon tumble from the eaves of the house, white wings glistening in the spring sunshine, she caught sight of Johnny's face at the nursery window, and remembered that over breakfast her aunt had mentioned that he was to visit little Victoria that morning to pronounce upon her health. Aunt Maria was hoping that the child could soon be released from isolation.

Johnny stared down, his face expressionless, then vanished. She sighed and walked on, pulling at the laurel leaves in restless discontent.

"Got you, my pretty maid!" crowed Tom, pouncing, his voice exultant at the success of his stalking.

She felt all her nerves jump in surprise and turned to find herself squeezed in a warm embrace, her waist encircled by Tom's arms, his face pushing against hers in an attempt at a kiss.

She indignantly demanded that he release her, trying without success to struggle free, her hands pushing at his shoulder.

"Only if you give me a kiss," he laughed, his face boyish with impudence.

"Certainly not!"

"Why not?" he asked, sulking.

"You are about to become betrothed, Tom," she pointed out, coldly.

"Oh, that!" he said, his lip stuck out obstinately.

"As if I give a fig for Charlotte! Why, I have known her all my life. She has a face like one of her horses."

"She seems very fond of you," said Sabrina, with reproach.

He had the grace to look uncomfortable. "Well, I am fond of her," he admitted crossly, "but it is hard to feel romantic about a girl who has ridden neck and neck with you over muddy country for half the day and then come home as fresh as she went out!"

"How un-sporting of her," she mocked, "to beat you!"

He flushed. "You may laugh, but I want to marry a girl with more of a sparkle. Charlotte is more like a brother than a girl one would care to marry."

"Well, you must marry her, and there is an end to it," she said coolly.

"Oh, Sabrina," he said, squeezing her tighter, his nose rubbing against her cheek, "be kind to me. Just one tiny kiss, and I swear I will let you go!"

"No," she said, shaking her head, "if you do not release me at once, I shall scream . . ."

"Spoil sport!" he sulked, dropping his hands, and, as she moved away, leaned forward and clumsily kissed her on the mouth.

Johnny's level voice spoke behind them, cold and formal, his words making Tom jump. "Wilton, will you go upstairs to the nursery and carry your little sister down to the morning room? I have given her permission to come down for one hour this morning."

Tom spun on his heels, reddening. He muttered something incoherent, shot Sabrina an uneasy glance, and walked away towards the house without another word.

Sabrina felt her throat tighten with shock and dismay. Pale, shivering as if with extreme cold, she stood, staring at Johnny.

His dark blue eyes were black with rage. Pale, tight-lipped, he said, "I warned you. You chose to ignore my warning. I suppose you believed yourself safe from me; you imagined you could twist me round your little finger as you did once before. Charlotte Colling is a fine girl, and I will not have her happiness threatened by you and that selfish boy. I said I would tell your aunt why you were dismissed from my uncle's house. And I will do so as soon as she returns from Epping. You shall not ruin Charlotte's life."

CHAPTER FOUR

"You do not know the whole truth," Sabrina cried passionately.

"The portion of it I do know is enough," he answered. "It is enough for me. It will be more than enough for your aunt. She is hardly likely to countenance immorality."

"You to talk of that," she said with bitterness. "What did you see? A kiss? Can you remember no occasion when you kissed me?"

His face reddened.

She waited and then said, "Or will all that be missing from your version of events?"

"Do you really imagine that your aunt would find it a justification that I, too, once kissed you? It would only confirm the truth of what I said. You would be condemning yourself out of hand. If you think otherwise, you are a fool."

His voice was as bitter as her own, his tone savage, taut.

She nodded, her lips twisted in pained admission. "Yes—a well brought up young lady never allows a gentleman to kiss her."

"Even," he said savagely, "when the gentleman is not married. And when he is married . . ."

"And you? Do you condemn me for kissing you? Are you quite blameless on that score?"

"As I remember the occasion," he said bitingly, "you were more than willing to be kissed."

Her hand flew up and slapped across his face, leaving a flat red stain on the side of his cheek. He started forward involuntarily, his teeth clenched, and for a moment she thought he would return the blow, but he drew himself in and stood there, his chin taut.

For a few moments, there was silence. Then, smiling thinly, he said, "Once again you almost made me forget I am a gentleman."

She laughed. "You? Does a gentleman tell tales? Sneak like a schoolboy?"

"Do you know," he said, in a light conversational style, turning away and gazing up at the sky, "you make me very angry sometimes. I thought I was extremely civilized, but you have taught me that I am capable of feeling a great deal of very uncivilized emotion." The words were carefully delivered in a soft voice, but his face was only just held in control, and the dark blue eyes held a hatred that made her feel sick.

She shivered. After a moment, she said, "And my sister? What of Charity?"

"Your sister does not enter into this," he retorted.

"Do you honestly imagine my aunt would let her stay? And if she had to leave, what is there for her? A post as a governess in some house where she is overworked, insulted, poorly paid? She is not fit for such a life."

"Your aunt is a kind woman," he returned, but uneasily. "She would not throw her out."

"Do you think Charity would stay here in such circumstances? That she could hear me accused and condemned, see me cast off, and stay? And if she could bring herself to do it, how would my aunt regard her? Tarred with the same brush, that is what people say. Whether she went or stayed, my sister would lead an unbearable life."

He turned on her savagely. "This is blackmail, moral blackmail!"

"It is the truth!"

He sneered. "The truth from you?"

"Yes, from me," she cried passionately. "And it was the truth that your uncle forced his attentions on me, that I did not invite or welcome them. The kiss you saw was the only one and would have always been so. You did not even give me the opportunity of explaining, of defending myself. You made up your mind and walked out."

"You were on his lap, your head on his shoulder," he burst out furiously. "You were hardly struggling! You looked, indeed, very comfortable and accustomed to your position!" His lips drew back from his teeth in a snarl, the dark blue eyes bored into hers. "I saw you! God damn you, I saw you, with my own eyes!"

"But I was taken by surprise," she said. "He suddenly seized me, and before I had a chance to do anything, you and your aunt came in . . ."

"Inconvenient of us," he drawled, drawing back, and his features smoothed out, all the angry emotion vanished.

"I tell you it is the truth," she cried, pleadingly.

"And I tell you it is a lie," he said. "Do you think I did not ask my uncle? I spoke to him next day. Point blank. I asked him if you were his mistress . . ."

She stared, eyes huge. In a parched voice, weary and drained, she asked, "And he said?"

"That you were, that you had been, for weeks."

"Oh!" She swayed, covering her face with her hands, "Oh, but it is not true." She looked up, still pleading, "You know it is not. Johnny, you must know. We . . . you and I . . ."

He laughed. "Oh, you and I! It would not be the first time such sleight of hand was practiced upon a fool in love. I suppose you saw me as a better long-term prospect? Was that it? I could marry you, and my uncle could not?"

"Why do you say such things? You cannot believe them!"

He caught her by the shoulders and shook her violently. "What did you get out of it? Did my uncle buy you the pretty things you wanted? Jewels was it? Or clothes? Or just plain, dull, very useful money?"

She shrank from the glare of his eyes, shivering, and he released her with a look of acute dislike.

White to the lips, she stared at the dark green leaves of the laurel, noticing the crystal rain drops caught and held in a cobweb which had been strung from stem to stem during the night. The sun sparkled on the fibers, giving them a brilliance which dazzled her eyes. She blinked and felt a wetness on her cheek. A tear ran down the corner of her mouth. A slight saltiness touched her inner lip, and she blinked to dispel the tears.

"I would be failing in my duty if I did not warn your aunt," Johnny said harshly.

She did not answer. Her throat was aching with the unshed tears she was holding back now.

"I should blame myself if you caused more harm here," he said, but his tone had quieted and was almost apologetic now.

"I would not care if it were just myself," she said wearily. "I am quite capable of earning enough to support myself. I would have chosen independence if it were not for my sister. Charity is so shy and nervous. She is just beginning to be happy here. If you had seen what her life was like with my father..."

He groaned. "Oh, very well. I will offer you a bargain. Leave here of your own free will, find a post somewhere. Then your sister may stay here, and no shame could attach to her."

Her face brightened. "Yes, yes, it might answer." Then she looked down. "But Charity would never forgive me; she would think I was deserting her. I promised to stay here with her."

"Find a post nearby. There are many large houses in the district."

"No," she said, her face thoughtful, then with a sudden smile, "No, I know what I will do! There is a post vacant in this very village."

"Here? At Ambreys, you mean? How will that accomplish..."

"No, the post of schoolmistress in Ambresbury."

"What? You cannot be serious!" He stared at her. "Your uncle would not permit it. His niece, teaching the urchins of Ambresbury? On his own doorstep? It is unthinkable."

"He will agree," she said, with conviction.

"It is impossible!"

"Ah, you think so, but I know the key to unlock that door," she said, half smiling.

He looked sharply at her. "What now?"

"My aunt," she said in triumph.

"I see. Yes, you may be right. She would be glad to be rid of you, and your uncle will be nagged to death until he agrees."

"And I shall give him such impeccable reasons for my decision," she said demurely. "And quite truthfully, I have often wished to be doing something of use in the world. It is my Christian duty to help the poor, and I shall be much better off than sitting idly here in luxury."

He put his hands in his pockets and rocked on his heels, his head to one side. "Yes, you will wheedle and confuse the poor man, I have no doubt. But I cannot see you living in that tiny cottage, teaching dolts of farm laborers' children. It is hardly the life to which you are accustomed."

"You know very little about me, though, do you?" she said sweetly, with a return of her usual spirit.

He shot her a half amused look. "You realize, I suppose, that the schoolhouse is opposite my own?"

"Then you will be able to keep an eye on me and be sure I am leading a respectable life," she said impudently, the relief of the reprieve making her daring.

"For that remark," he said grimly, "you deserve to be birched."

"You are right," she observed softly. "Your civilized exterior is only skin deep."

He glared at her, and she went on quickly, "I do not believe in the birch for children, in any case."

"You will," he said, "if you are serious in taking on this position. Some of those lads are only to be cowed by the birch."

"I shall not want to cow them," she retorted. "I have theories of my own about the education of children."

He laughed, "Have you, by Heaven? You amaze me." For a moment their eyes met, smiling, and then he drew back, frowning, as if annoyed with himself.

"Well, it is a bargain," he said crisply. "You leave Ambreys, and I keep your secret."

"Agreed," she said, and they walked back to the house together in silence, shaking hands in the hall, under the interested eyes of the butler, with great politeness.

Sabrina tackled her aunt on the next day. "You? Schoolmistress of Ambresbury?" Aunt Maria stared in absolute amazement, and then began to laugh. "Silly child! What an idea!"

Sabrina talked quickly, softly, allowing her aunt to see all the implications. "With Tom soon to be married, and Louisa to bring out, you are so busy that I feel I am imposing on your kindness. And I have a great wish to do something useful, to awaken young minds, to teach them how to lead good lives . . . A Christian act of compassion . . . I am deeply grateful to you, but . . . I believe I would be doing the right thing . . . Tom's betrothal and Louisa's coming out . . ." she went over the ideas again and again, watching her aunt.

Aunt Maria attempted to control her expression, but her thoughts were clear in her face. Were Sabrina, with her dazzling red hair and her spirited mind, out of the house, Tom would more easily fall into line, and Louisa could shine unopposed. Charity, dear sweet child, was no problem. The seeds took root, flourished, grew.

Aloud she said, coming to the heart of the problem, "But your uncle would never hear of it."

"If we both spoke to him," Sabrina urged. "If he knew how eager I am to be of use to the community? That I feel it my Christian duty? A sacred charge?"

Aunt Maria stared at her, shaking her head. "Are you truly in earnest?" she asked, incredulously, unable to believe that a girl with Sabrina's enchanting good looks could wish to immolate herself in a schoolhouse in a village.

"I am," said Sabrina, and knew it to be true. She had first conceived the idea in desperation, but on closer reflection, had grown quite serious about it, drawn to the idea of performing some useful task, of being fully occupied for once in her life, instead of carrying messages and running errands for her aunt.

Aunt Maria said slowly, "After dinner tonight would be the best time . . ."

"Yes," said Sabrina, quick to understand, and they looked at each other in mutual satisfaction.

Aunt Maria tackled him alone. "What? My niece teaching in a village school? As if she were Miss Nobody from Nowhere? Teaching the riff-raff of Ambresbury? I never heard such moonshine in my life."

His wife spoke softly again, and he threw up his hands. "I want to hear no more, Maria! The girl is demented."

But he was forced to hear more. Day after day,

Sabrina and her aunt labored to bring him to see their viewpoint. At length, in weary resignation, he said, "Heaven alone knows what the county will say! I shall be the laughing stock of the neighborhood."

"Surely it is a worthy ambition to improve the lot of the poor," said Sabrina. "Why should they laugh?"

"Oh, yes, all very fine for the lower orders," he said, sighing, "but you are my niece, girl. Cannot you see how it will look to my friends?"

And to his wife, when they were alone, "I put this down to her father's quirky nature. He was one of those Quakers, you know. Fanatical sort of fellow. Long-faced, preaching chap. Never knew what my poor sister saw in him."

"Well," said his wife contentedly, "at least she will be out of Tom's path. We must make quite sure he never goes down to the village alone."

Her husband eyed her. "Ah, Tom, is it? I wondered what bee had got into your bonnet, Maria!"

"Do you want him to marry Charlotte, or don't you?" she retorted tartly.

"He has more sense than to spoil his chances by a fling with his cousin," said his father.

"Has he?" Aunt Maria demanded. "He cannot take his eyes off her. And Tom has no more sense than any other man where a pretty girl is concerned."

Her husband was silenced.

Sabrina was forced to suffer much other amazement, comment, disbelief.

Louisa stared at her, "Teach those dirty little things? You cannot be serious! You will very likely catch some horrid disease. They are alive with lice, and I daresay have never had a bath in their lives. I would not sit in the same room with them for five minutes."

"They have souls," said Sabrina, "and need our help."

"Leave that to Mr. Frazer," Louisa retorted. "He is paid to preach to the poor."

"He cannot teach them to sew, read and count," Sabrina said.

"Why should they need to learn such things? They had far better go out to work."

"Little children, younger than Victoria?"

"They always have done—why change things? It will only lead to trouble."

Sabrina shrugged and left her.

Charity was equally incredulous, with different reason. "I agree that the poor children need help, but why you? There are many others more qualified and needing to be employed."

"I wish to do this, Charity," Sabrina said gently.

Charity stared at her, but her father's training forced her to accept her sister's decision at its face value. "Very well," she said, in resignation, "I shall come, too."

Sabrina spoke firmly, with the gentlest tinge of reproach, "And leave poor Aunt Maria, just when she will need you most? With Tom about to be betrothed, and Louisa coming out, and Victoria still very delicate? I did not think it of you, Charity."

"You cannot live alone," said Charity, shocked.

"I shall not do so," Sabrina said. "I am to have a little maid. Uncle Matthew is to pay for her keep, and I am to choose her from the village girls." She hugged Charity, "We will see each other often, dear.

It is only a step from the village. You shall come and have tea with me. Think—my own little house! Such grandeur!"

Charity was not so easily pacified, however, and it took time for Sabrina to talk her into staying at Ambreys alone. Trained to do her duty, to expect little, she had not sufficient selfishness to accept that her present happy life at Ambreys could be the right choice. Sabrina had to be patient, gentle, firm for days before Charity was silenced.

During that time, Sabrina was busy with preparations for her new life. She had to choose furniture from the store in the attics, select a maid from the girls sent up to Ambreys to be interviewed, arrange an opening date for the school, be interviewed herself by a curious, disbelieving, half shocked education board, and, finally, work out a syllabus which was suitable for the children to be placed in her charge.

She was a girl of energy and strength of character whose mind had never been stretched to anything like its capacity. Half of her energy had lain untapped for years. Domestic work barely scraped the surface of her mind. She could perform those tasks without using her brain, and she had a strong, powerful mind, capable of much more demanding exertion than it had hitherto been called upon to undertake.

Her energies lay waiting to be released, and, as she began to consider her future life, she became increasingly interested.

The maid she chose was a girl of twelve years called Molly Duckett, whose fresh coloring and bright eyes gave her a pleasant look of health and cheerfulness.

"I've seven brothers and sisters at home, Miss. And I've always had to help my Mam. I can cook, sew, clean, do anything that's needed, even kill fowls or make candles with mutton fat."

"Is your mother content to have you leave home, Molly?" Sabrina asked. "How will she manage without you?"

"We needs the money, Miss," the girl said simply. "Too many mouths to feed."

"I see." Sabrina studied her with a sympathetic smile. "Well, I will try you, Molly. I shall provide your clothes. You know your salary?"

"Yes, Miss," Molly nodded ecstatically, "five pounds a year paid quarterly."

"Good. Can you read and write?"

"I can write my name," Molly said with cautious assurance.

"No more?"

The girl looked defensive. "No, Miss. But I can cook, and clean, and . . ."

"Yes, I know. Well, I shall teach you to read and write in the evenings, Molly, and perhaps your father could send one of your brothers to school, too."

Molly gave her a pitying glance. "At twopence a week, Miss? We're lucky if we has enough to eat every day. Boots and clothes is hard to find when you only earn one and sixpence a day. My Pa, he's a good cowman, he is, been with Mr. Link fifteen year and more, but nobody earns more than one and sixpence on Sweet Briars. My Pa grows vegetables, and we keeps hens, and every year we gets a piglet from the farm to fatten, but money isn't made of elastic."

Sabrina sighed. "Well, I shall teach you, and perhaps you could teach your sisters a little." And she took the child down to the kitchen and told the cook to find her a parcel of food to take home. She saw Molly, from her bedroom, walking round the stables, a big basket of bread, eggs and cold meat under her arm, her rosy face one huge smile, and sighed again. Poor child, she thought, remembering her own luxurious breakfast. How many bowls of scraps went out from the kitchens of Ambreys, she wondered? The enormous meals, prepared at such expense and consumed by so few, with so much wastage at the end! It was shameful.

Byrd Johnstone, when he heard about her decision, rode over to express his amazement and protest vigorously, "You cannot do it," he said firmly.

"But I shall," she smiled, her chin set obstinately.

"It is unbelievable that your uncle could permit it," he said. "I understand that your father had strange views . . ."

"My father would undoubtedly have disapproved," she said, smiling. "He was a conventional man, despite Uncle Matthew's opinion of him."

He looked hard at her. They had met on a number of occasions now, and she was aware that he paid her distinguishing attention. Her uncle had even hinted at a possible marriage in the future, and now she felt a sudden flash of intuition. He was, she felt sure, on the point of making a premature declaration. He began hurriedly, "If you feel unhappy here at Ambreys . . ."

She broke in before he could go on. "I am not unhappy here, but I feel I must do some useful work. I want to be near my sister, but employed and busy . . ."

"You are a strange girl," he said, shaking his head. "I do not understand you."

She rode down to the village with him that day, on various errands for her aunt, and he patiently waited at each gate as she delivered the parcel of red flannel, the book, the bottle of home made wine, to each house. Aunt Maria was loath to hear of anyone crossing the threshold without having some useful office to perform.

They met Tom on their way back, and he persuaded them to ride along one of the forest paths for a while.

Byrd Johnstone was not pleased at Tom's arrival, but he consented, saying to Sabrina, "I hope that your new duties will not put an end to our rides together."

"The board have settled that there is to be no school on Saturday afternoon or Sunday," she said, "so I shall have free time for myself. But I do not know if my uncle will permit me to continue to borrow his horses."

"Of course he will, Sabrina," said Tom cheerfully.

"Sabrina," said Mr. Johnstone softly, "such a very pretty name. And unusual. I never met anyone called Sabrina before."

"Her father stole it from a poem," Tom told him. "It's Latin."

Mr. Johnstone glanced sideways at him, his expression wry, "I know the poem," he said, and quoted softly, "Sabrina fair, listen where thou art sitting, under the glassy, cool, translucent wave . . ."

Tom stared at him. "I never knew you were bookish, before, Byrd," he said scornfully.

Mr. Johnstone laughed. And Sabrina, listening to them, smiled, staring up at the new green of the trees, the sun shafting through to light their path, and felt strangely happy.

"Look, Mr. Johnstone," she said suddenly, "a squirrel . . ."

He looked and smiled. "The forest is full of them. They are just out of hibernation, I suppose." Then, as Tom paused to watch the squirrel, aiming an imaginary gun at the pretty beast, he edged his horse closer, and said, "I hope you did not object when I used your name just now. Your cousin uses it so freely, and the sound is so pretty . . ."

She smiled at him. "Please call me Sabrina if you wish."

He looked pleased. "And will you call me Byrd? Your family will not think it too forward on such short acquaintance?"

"My family and I are soon to part," she said lightly. "I think I may safely say I am old enough to have charge of my own name."

When they rode back to Ambreys, they met Johnny on the portico, about to leave after a visit to Victoria, now fully recovered from her childish ailment. He bowed in silence, his glance resting on Sabrina only a second, and she felt a pang of disappointment that she had not been at home when he came. She had not seen him since the day they had struck their bargain in the shrubberies.

Victoria, a plump, cheerful child with her brother's self assurance, asked Sabrina that afternoon if she liked Byrd Johnstone. "He likes you," she declared with the usual directness of a child. "I saw him staring at you this morning. Shall you marry him, Sabrina, and not be a schoolmistress?"

Her mother cried, "Victoria! Be silent!" But her own glance was curious and a little jealous, as she said it.

Sabrina smiled and did not answer. She liked Byrd Johnstone and found his company pleasant, but she knew that she could never love him, and, for her, that made any closer relationship out of the question.

I must see as little of him as possible, she thought, bending over her sewing. Any other course would be grossly unfair to him. She had, of course, observed his interest in her, and been flattered by it, but for the present her new life as schoolmistress of Ambresbury would, she thought, content her.

Her uncle and the rest of the board had decided to wait until the end of the summer before opening the school. The children would be fulfilling their ancient role of crop-defenders and harvesters until the autumn. Even little girls of five could be trusted to stand in the fields and scare the birds, and boys of eight or nine could perform many little tasks around the farms. There was great opposition to the new school from the farmers already, foreseeing a shortage of cheap child labor in the fields, and the board thought it would be wisest to wait until the fieldwork was more scarce before opening the school.

But Sabrina still had a great deal to do before the school could be said to be ready, and, with her uncle's permission, Molly moved into the school-house to make it habitable, and air the damp rooms before Sabrina herself arrived.

Sabrina began to spend a great deal of her time there, driving down in the trap alone, arousing the curiosity of the villagers as she drove past at a spanking trot.

One bright May morning, she arrived and paused in the little garden to gaze around with pride. Uncle Matthew had sent one of his men down to tend the garden. There was now a thin sprinkling of grass to be seen on the square lawn. Wallflowers, orange and rusty red, were bedded tightly in rows, their heavy scent filling the air. Dew still glistened in their dark hearts.

Molly flew to open the door, beaming at her. "Bright and early again, Miss," she said, ushering her in with pride.

The furniture was mostly of the late eighteenth century, delicate and gilded, with a beautifully balanced proportion in the lines.

Aunt Maria apologized, "Ugly old-fashioned stuff, my dear, but it is still serviceable . . ."

"I like it," Sabrina had assured her. "It is very elegant . . ."

Her aunt had smiled at her, "Such a kind girl . . ." she had murmured, a little shame-faced.

The house was tiny, a doll's house, with two bedrooms and one small parlor, a kitchen and a dark, poky wash house, which Molly regarded as her greatest treasure.

"No more wet washing slapping me in the face, Miss! I can hang it all out here and keep the kitchen free of it. I do hate wet washing. At home, on wet days we can hardly walk about for it."

Now it was neat, ordered, snug, in the doll's house. Book shelves had been built into the chimney corner. Cozy chairs stood on either side of the hearth. Glass and china were displayed in a wooden dresser which stood along one wall. Everything shone, polished out of existence, and a fire burned in the parlor grate.

"It was cold as death in here, Miss," Molly said. "I thought a fire would be nice for you even on a nice day like this."

They inspected the kitchen. Molly poked the fire with zest, rattling the grate to release the ashes. "I can run this house easy as pie," she said, pushing the hob round so that the kettle came to rest above the fire. "I'll have a pot of tea for you in a minute. Why don't you go and sit down by the fire?"

Sabrina regarded her with misgivings. She was such a young girl to have so much work to do. But Molly's motherly air made her smile, and she submitted to the child's gentle tyranny with amused warmth.

When Molly brought the heavy tray through to the parlor, Sabrina ordered her to sit down. "I am going to read to you," she said.

Molly was shocked. "Sit down? Me, Miss? Oh, I couldn't. Not in my dirty clothes."

"Your clothes are perfectly clean," Sabrina said. "Take off your apron and sit down."

Molly began to argue, was checked, and obeyed

with a frown of disapproval, laying her thick sacking apron on a chair as if it were armor.

Sabrina reached down a book of fairy tales and began to read one aloud. Molly listened, wide-eyed, her face changing gradually, wonder, excitement, fear, delight alternating in her features. When Sabrina came to an end, the child gave a deep sigh. "You do read lovely, Miss. Better than Parson. He uses too many long words, and he mutters, so I never understand half what he says."

Someone laughed softly behind them, and Molly sprang up, giving a cry of panic.

Johnny walked forward into the room. "I did knock, but there was no answer," he said, smiling at Molly. "I came round to the back door."

The child fled past him, snatching up her apron and tying it on with clumsy fingers as she dived into her kitchen and closed the door.

"Well," Johnny said, "how do you like your new abode? I have watched the transformation with much interest. You have made it a very comfortable home."

"Thank you," she said, very conscious of him in this tiny room.

He strolled over and sat down, stretching out his hands to the blaze. "I did not believe you would go through with it. I congratulate you."

She flushed. "I am grateful to you for giving me the idea. I might have missed the fun of having something to work and plan towards."

"Is it fun?" he asked curiously, watching her.

"Yes," she said, "it is the most exciting thing to happen to me in my life."

His lips twisted wryly. "Is it indeed?" he asked,

oddly grimacing. "Well, well, well. Why, exactly?"

"I am not sure. I suppose because I have responsibility, independence . . . Oh, a great many things I never had before."

"You were a governess, before," he said.

"Yes," she admitted, "but in a difficult position. Your aunt did not believe in education and was only interested in having her daughters learn to play the piano, embroider, sing . . ."

"And what will you teach these country girls, then?" he asked.

"I shall teach them a number of things," she said, "chiefly, to think for themselves."

"Good God," he shouted, "would you undermine society? You might as well teach them to be Chartists . . ."

She shook her head. "Will you have tea? Molly just made it freshly . . ."

He watched her as she poured, his gaze abstracted. Then he leaned back, his eyes half closed, and stared at the fire. "This is very comfortable," he said. "My house is like an army barracks. I have a village woman who comes in by day. She seems to believe it is a crime to be comfortable. She cooks me leaden puddings and soggy cabbage, and complains if I do not eat them."

She watched him, his face relaxed, the skin lying at rest over his cheekbones, his lids flickering in the heat of the flames. He looked more at ease than he had ever done since they met again.

For a moment, she thought he had gone to sleep, then his lids drew back, and he looked at her. "We must come to an understanding, Sabrina. We cannot see each other every day and remain in a state of armed hostility. Shall we begin again?"

Dry-mouthed, she said, "Yes," and could find no breath to say more.

He glanced back to the fire. "Do not misunderstand me. I am not able to forget the past. We shall be working together with these children; we shall often be in company. That is all I mean. We cannot work together with the past continually between us. We must push it aside, swear a truce."

"I understand," she said, disappointment aching inside her.

He looked at her again, sharply, "Do you? I am not going back to where we were, Sabrina. This is a new beginning, but I am going to begin from a new starting point. We shall be colleagues. No more than that. I want that understood."

"It is understood," she said coolly.

He stared at her for a moment. "Good," he said, oddly, "I am glad we understand each other."

She wondered why his eyes were narrowed, his face unsmiling. Did he still suspect her intentions? she thought. Well, she would show him his suspicions were groundless. Johnny would never have cause to claim that she had not kept her side of the bargain.

CHAPTER FIVE

One of her new pupils, she discovered, was to be the eight-year-old daughter of the tenant of White Briars, her uncle's largest farm. The child was pretty and pert, her manners more forward than Sabrina found pleasant. She visited the schoolhouse with her mother to add her name to the school list, and Mrs. Link lost no time in asserting social claims by inviting Sabrina to the farm for tea. Having observed the insolence with which Mrs. Link treated Molly, Sabrina was not sorry to refuse, politely, pleading a press of business.

"And I think it might be unwise to single out your family," she added quietly. "Relations are always sensitive in a village. Other parents might suspect some favoritism."

Mrs. Link, stiff and flushed, withdrew, but her parting glance was distinctly unfriendly, and Molly eyed her mistress, grinning.

"Nasty old toad," she murmured.

"Molly, mind your manners! You must not make personal remarks."

Molly made sketchy movements of domestic business, then, her back turned, said, "She's always boasting round the village how she's come down in the world. Her father was a sailor, she says; a captain,

87

no less. She says! She reckons she's a lady. The airs she puts on! Enough to make a cat laugh."

"Molly, be quiet!" said Sabrina, wondering how she was to run her new household when she found it so hard to silence her maid! It was so easy to listen, laugh, treat her with indulgence. So bright and cheerful a child was easy to grow attached to, but she was aware that she must make some pretense of discipline.

Molly continued to talk of the Links, undeterred. "Emily's their only one," she said; "Mr. Link would like to have a son, but they say Mrs. Link is past it."

"Molly!" Sabrina's voice was seriously affronted now, "leave this room at once!"

With a whisk of her skirts and an unrepentant twinkle, Molly obeyed.

Molly's claims to be a cook, it appeared, had been somewhat exaggerated in the telling. She boiled everything she could, throwing the vegetables and meat together into a pot and reducing them to a thick brown glue by hours of cooking. She had no knowledge of sauces or pastry, but made excellent, if strong, tea, and on tea and bread and butter, Sabrina mainly existed.

Since she found it so hard to speak to the child, Sabrina was forced to listen to her unending gossip, and, despite herself, was fascinated by this revelation of the hidden side of village life. Molly knew everything. It was from her that Sabrina learned that Johnny was idolized by the villagers. Many of them had had treatment without any fee being tendered. He never refused to see a patient, however poor, and would come out in all weathers to visit the sick.

"They find something for him, though," Molly said with satisfaction, "some onions, or a hare, or a bowl of pickled walnuts."

Amused by the idea of Johnny, weighed down with onions and pickled walnuts, trotting round the lanes in his trap, Sabrina listened, disguising her smile. It gave her pleasure to hear him spoken of with such honest admiration.

One day when she met him, she asked, "Why did you come to Ambresbury, Johnny?"

He had looked sharply at her, reddening a little, "Why? I was sick of London, I suppose, and I wished to be nearer my brother. He was just ill enough, then, to warrant concern, although I believed it to be no more than a general weakness of the chest. I hoped that with proper care and a sensible regime, he might recover." He sighed. "But he grew worse. And when I called in a specialist, he recommended Switzerland."

"How is your brother now?" she asked gently.

His face was somber. "The reports are not hopeful."

She wondered what he would do when he inherited Dancing Hill. He would have to give up medicine and settle to the life of a squire, she imagined.

They paused at her gate. Byrd was there before them, on his big black stallion, leading the bay gelding she usually rode now. Johnny tipped his hat with a muttered word of goodbye, crossed the road and slammed into his cottage.

She and Byrd rode several times a week, sometimes in company with Uncle Matthew, or another member of the family, sometimes alone. Sabrina found Byrd a comforting companion. His manner was easy and pleasant, his mind surprisingly quick to follow her own. He somehow found time to read a good deal and, although not an intellectual, was very intelligent. Their conversations covered a good deal of ground, and their views were often similar.

Tom had been sent away to Scotland to stay with a cousin, and Aunt Maria smiled favorably upon Sabrina's rides with Byrd, especially since they removed her from the house for hours at a time. She had even bought Sabrina a new riding habit, a gay dark blue one which Sabrina wore with reluctance, since she was officially still in mourning. But, "It is near enough to black," Aunt Maria insisted.

Johnny was a frequent visitor to Ambreys. The subject of his brother's health obsessed Aunt Maria. Daily bulletins were sought and discussed with a show of deep concern which disgusted Sabrina, knowing as she did that her aunt's real concern was for the length of time which must elapse before Johnny inherited Dancing Hill and became an eligible suitor for Louisa.

Sabrina watched him with Louisa, trying to decide how he felt about her cousin, but although he treated her with undoubted teasing attention, she could not be sure whether this was due to real attraction, or was just his manner towards a young, very shy girl.

Of course, Louisa would be an excellent match. Uncle Matthew could afford to be generous with her dowry. But her personal attractions were so limited, her manner so clumsy and sullen, that Sabrina could not believe Johnny to be seriously pursuing her.

As to Louisa, herself, her feelings towards him

were easier to estimate since she confided in Charity to some extent, and by her blushes and awkwardness made her own preference only too clear. But that it was the preference of a surface attraction, Sabrina was convinced. Louisa was too inward-looking to be capable of a deep affection. Her childish sulkiness had diminished but not disappeared.

One Saturday afternoon in early June, Sabrina was preparing some boxes of silks for the school, when she heard a commotion in the street. She looked out of the window and saw Molly flying towards her, her apron to her eyes, weeping noisily.

Sabrina ran to the door. "What is it? What has happened?"

"Rob fell out of the yew tree," Molly sobbed. "His arm is broke. I'm going to get Dr. Graham." And she fled across the road.

Sabrina ran down to the churchyard and found a little crowd chattering by the gate. Under the yew, one arm lying at an unnatural angle, lay Rob, Molly's eight-year-old brother, his face white, groaning and sobbing for his mother.

"Is he dead, Miss?" one child asked her avidly, and the village women burst out with loud explanations as she arrived.

"His head is broken . . ."

"He did fall hard . . . is his neck broke? Oooh, listen to him scream . . ."

Rob, his eyes screwed tight, was indeed screaming, and Sabrina could not blame him. The excited gloom around him was terrifying him. She firmly shooed all the onlookers away, shutting the gate behind them, and returned to Rob. Gently, she stroked the hair out of his eyes. "Doctor Graham will be here soon, Rob, and you are going to be a brave boy. You have broken your arm, but you will get better very soon."

His bag in his hand, Johnny jumped over the wall at that moment and knelt down by Rob, smiling at him. "What have you been up to, my lad? You should have been a monkey, climbing trees like that."

"I broke me arm, Doctor," said the boy with a pitiful attempt at a smile.

Sabrina stood up to move away, and Rob's eyes flew to her. "Miss, Miss, don't go away . . ." he begged.

Johnny shot her a look, his brows raised. "Miss is going to stay, Rob," he said, gently examining the boy's arm. "Now, I am afraid I must carry you back to my house to attend to this arm, so will you be brave a while longer?"

"My house is nearer," Sabrina said. "It will hurt him less to be carried there."

Johnny nodded. "Thank you." He gently lifted the boy, who groaned and bit his lip, and they crossed the churchyard to the School House.

Molly and Sabrina made a pot of tea and gave Rob a cup, black and very sweet, laced with brandy which Uncle Matthew had given Sabrina for medicinal purposes. Rob grimaced but swallowed it, and by the time Johnny was ready to attend to him, the boy was lying sleepily against the pillows Sabrina had put behind his head. Johnny bent over him and caught the odor of the brandy. He looked up, his eyes twinkling. "How much did you give him?"

"Half a cupful," she admitted.

His brows flew up. "Good heavens! He'll be drunk for a week!"

Sabrina held the boy while Johnny deftly bandaged the arm. During the previous handling, Rob had been jerked out of his drowsiness into agony, but now he lay, pale but relieved, watching Johnny.

"I shall have to drive him home," Johnny said absently.

And when he returned with his trap to drive the boy back to his home, Sabrina told him that she was going too, "To hold Rob's head," she said.

Johnny grimaced oddly. "Very well," he said. Molly carried an armful of cushions out to the trap while Johnny carried the boy. He laid him in Sabrina's lap, the thin legs, in their torn trousers, dangling against her full skirts. Rob opened his eyes to smile at her. Pain shadowed his small face, but his smile was impudent. "You going to cuddle me, Miss?"

She laughed. "Would you mind, Rob?"

"Not me," he said cheerfully, nestling against her.

Johnny was watching them, his face expressionless. "Ready?" he asked.

She nodded, and they set off, Molly waving her handkerchief from the gate.

The sky was a bright blue overhead, but to the east dark clouds were banking up, drifting slowly towards them before a chill wind.

"Going to rain," Johnny said over his shoulder. "I hope we get the boy home before it breaks."

When they reached the cottage, Mrs. Duckett came out slowly. She pushed back limp hair from her forehead, staring at them. Her body was distorted by pregnancy, her face sallow and unwashed, but she held out her arms to Rob at once.

"Oh, what now?" she wailed as she took him.

"A broken arm, Mrs. Duckett," said Johnny. "He'll live."

"You bad boy," she scolded Rob. "Oh, Doctor, he should have been scaring the crows off Five Acre Field today. Farmer Link has been down in a terrible great rage. Says he'll flay the hide off him. As if I haven't enough to worry about..."

They carried him into the tiny house. Sabrina looked round in dismay and pity. Did so many human beings live in this filthy, cramped place? The cottage was half as big as hers, the stairs were open treads, without handrail or support, leading up to a small room, with cracked and dirty plaster walls, floors of splintered wood, the roof beams wreathed in cobwebs.

"He'll get it from his Da when he comes home," wailed Mrs. Duckett, laying Rob on the bed and covering him with a stained blanket.

"Since our Molly left home, I can't seem to get things done," wailed Mrs. Duckett as they returned downstairs. She sank into a chair and stared around her listlessly. There were vegetables on the table, covered in mud, waiting to be prepared. A huge wooden tub stood by the fire with clothes soaking in it, and a dog lay nearby, scratching vigorously. The house was in total disarray.

"Would you like Molly to come home for a while?" Sabrina asked gently. "I can manage without her until your baby is born."

Mrs. Duckett stared at her, open-mouthed. "Oh, I dursent," she said.

Sabrina had never heard the expression before, and was baffled.

Johnny translated. "She is afraid to accept." He glanced at the woman. "Your husband?"

"He'd lam into me," she nodded. "He says I don't try, but just let someone else have a go. Seven children to feed and care for, and a man to run after, and me expecting another . . . It isn't easy, Doctor."

"It is not," he agreed gently.

They left in a moment, and Johnny returned, ostensibly to speak to Mrs. Duckett, but Sabrina saw him quite clearly handing the woman some money, and saw Mrs. Duckett scrubbing at her eyes as he hurried out.

A warmth invaded her. When he joined her, she smiled at him, feeling as proud as if she had a right to feel pride in him, and deciding to send Molly home next day with food for the family and some flannel for the coming baby's clothes.

They drove back to Ambresbury in silence, but half a mile down the road a man hailed them from a field. Johnny halted the trap and bade him a good day.

"I have just been visiting one of your cottages. Young Rob Duckett. Broke his arm. He will not be fit for work for weeks, I am afraid."

The farmer came down on to the road, scowling, his broad shoulders lifted in irritation. He was a man of forty or so, black haired and heavy-browed. "Damn that boy! So that was where he was, gallivanting about! I'll stop his wages, the young devil!"

"There's a lady present, Link," Johnny said coldly.

The farmer stared at Sabrina, his black eyes bold and insolent, "Yes, I saw her. New schoolmistress, eh? Heard of her from my wife."

"Miss Crammond," said Johnny pointedly, "is the Squire's niece."

Link sneered. "Aye, I've heard. Wouldn't let a niece of mine teach that rabble. What use is schooling to them, pray? I've said and I'll say it again, the school should be for the farmers' children only. I don't want my Emily sitting next to dirty brats like the Duckett children."

"The Duckett children cannot afford to pay twopence a week for schooling," Sabrina said angrily.

"And just as well! If God intended people like that to have schooling, he would have given them brains, and no Duckett has ever had brains. A parcel of ne'er do wells, the Ducketts."

"And perhaps if they had education, they would not be content to work for a pittance, Mr. Link," Sabrina said tartly.

His heavy face reddened slowly, and he stared at her with furious eyes. "I pay the same wages as every other farmer around here," he said, his voice raised, "and even at that, I nearly bankrupt myself. I only just manage to stagger on from year to year, scraping by. Harvest was bad again last year. Prices are rock bottom. If they do not go up this year, I shall have to turn some men off soon."

"I hope you will not have to do so then," Johnny said soberly. "There is no work for men for miles, Link. I hate to see families driven into the workhouse for want of work."

"Squire wants his rent just the same, Doctor, whether I have the money or not, and why should I be different? I'm not in farming for the pleasure of it; I'm in it to make money. I have a family to support. And at least the paupers don't starve in the workhouse. Better there than die of starvation in the open ditches."

"Some of them might prefer that," said Sabrina, shivering at the very idea of that grim place.

He stared at her, his jowls purple. "You've never known hunger, Miss, or you wouldn't say that. Anything is better than starving. And I pay my rates, same as everyone else. I expect to have my turned off men cared for by the Union."

"Our nearest workhouse is Epping Union," Johnny explained to her.

"At Theydon Garnon," Mr. Link interrupted, nodding, "a bit of a step from here. A handsome building it is, too, cost a great deal of public money. Eight thousand pounds, they do say, and room for three hundred paupers. Built only five years, too. What more could they want? They get food, a roof over their heads. They should thank God for it."

"How many will you turn off?" Johnny asked.

Mr. Link stared at Sabrina with hostility, "The Ducketts must go, for one. Too many of them for my liking. A poor man has no right to have so many children." He wiped his face with his handkerchief and looked up at the sky. "Bad weather on the way. I must get on. Good day to you, Doctor." He looked at Sabrina with dislike. "Good day to you, Miss."

Sabrina stared after him. "What a very unpleasant man," she said, shuddering.

"He's hard," Johnny agreed, "but he is right, farming is in a bad way. And that means more and more homeless paupers in Epping Workhouse."

"The Ducketts, though, all those children . . ."

"Yes," Johnny sighed, "do you know the father, Will Duckett?"

"No," she said.

"He is a proud man. The Workhouse would drive him to madness. It haunts them, you know, day and night. I have seen strong men turn white at the very name. Their spirits are broken. They lose self respect rapidly. Stop washing. Stop eating. Die of sheer lack of will to survive in that place. It is worse than a prison, because at least with prison, you may hope to get out, and you know why you are there. With the workhouse, despair is their constant companion."

Then he looked up. "We must hurry before that storm breaks. There is little shelter along this road until you reach the forest."

They drove along a winding lane, heavy with the scent of hawthorn, the banks lacy with floating white petals, scattered on the approaching wind.

The rain began falling, in soft drops, and the wind blew fiercely. She looked up with apprehension, and saw the heart of the storm clouds over their heads, dark and menacing, the edges shining with a livid glow. A sudden flash made her start. The horse plunged nervously and Johnny turned to look at her.

"We must drive off the road into the forest!" he shouted, whipping up the horse.

The forest loomed up round the corner and Johnny drew the trap to a standstill under some great oaks which leaned down over the road. "In here . . ." he panted, and tethered the horse to a thick branch before running up the bank and turning to aid her.

Wet and breathing hard, she joined him under the leafy canopy. "Where are we?"

"Ambresbury Banks," he said, pointing behind them, to where a succession of earth banks rose and fell, oak and hornbeam growing from them.

"The old British camp?" she asked in surprise and some disappointment.

"You've heard of it?"

"My father mentioned it," she admitted, staring across the forest.

In the moats between each bank of earth grew ferns, dark green and smelling of water. The ground was black and fibrous. Twisted roots snaked down the sides of the banks, holding them against erosion, and soft pockets of moss lay here and there, growing where grass could not, careless of the lack of light under the thickly planted trees.

The wind, whining through the branches, made the ancient hornbeams writhe, like human beings in agony, their old wood rattling in mimicry of death. They were dry and sere, bent double with the years, their leaves few and tattered. Powerful young beech trees were thrusting in among them, elbowing them out of the way, and the insidious holly pricked their flanks.

"It isn't much to look at," Johnny said idly, gazing around.

"It has an eerie atmosphere in this light, though," she said, shivering, and, indeed, as the lightning flashed down through the gloomy half light under the trees, the Banks took on a rather frightening aspect.

"The locals will never come here at night," Johnny said. "They are convinced that you can see the ghost fires of the Iceni flickering among the trees, the camp fires of Boadicea and her tribe. Now and then some late straggler comes running home, screaming that he has seen the ghost fires or heard the death cries of the Iceni, but I'd swear to it, it is only the wind they heard, or the glow of a woodman's fire."

Sabrina pressed back against the trees, her eyes searching the darkness. The rain still fell in torrents; she could see it stream past in the wind, and the thunder crashed overhead, making her start and tremble. Somewhere in the forest a branch fell, cracking and crashing against other trees.

"Why, you are white," Johnny said, turning to her. "Are you frightened?"

"A little," she admitted, in a voice rusty with fear.

He smiled at her. "You are quite safe in here, you know. The safest place in the world. There are a thousand trees for the lightning to choose. They stretch for miles. You need not be afraid it will choose the one we are sheltering under."

His closeness and gentleness calmed her. He leaned against the tree, his shoulder touching hers, talking softly about the forest, and she watched his lean face and dark blue eyes, their expression changing from moment to moment, his glance now and then flying to her face.

A warm pleasure slowly grew inside her. She noticed the motion of his lips as he spoke, the droop of his lids, the pull of the muscles in his cheek, the small laughter lines running from the corner of his eyes and mouth. We are shut in together, she thought, in this dark forest, with the wind drawing a curtain of rain around us. There is no living soul for miles, and Johnny is smiling at me.

Her eyes lifted to his face, she gazed at him, and he turned to smile at her before she had time to withdraw her glance or disguise its meaning.

His smile vanished, the dark blue eyes widened, and she saw his nostrils flare with some sudden emotion. Slowly he put out a hand and touched her cheek, tipping up her chin towards him.

Dry-mouthed, she watched as his head bent closer. The hunger which had been growing inside her over the last few minutes, burned fiercely; she involuntarily put her hands up to his shoulders, her fingers curling as they touched the damp cloth of his coat.

His lips almost touched hers, her lids fell, her head tipped back against the solid trunk of the great oak.

But his mouth did not touch hers, and after a moment, her eyes opened again, to find him staring at her, brows drawn together, his expression contemptuous.

"No," he said softly, "oh, no, I am not to be caught twice in the same trap."

She flushed, trembled, went white. Her eyes fell to the sodden ground below the bank on which they stood, where little runnels of water trickled along the hard, root-ribbed earth.

The rain had slowed. After another moment, it ceased altogether. In the forest the rain still dripped from leaf to leaf with a steady rhythm.

In silence they went out to the trap and found it awash with rain. Johnny swept the worst out, with a fallen branch, and then wiped the seat with his handkerchief.

He avoided her eyes as he lifted her into the trap, climbed up himself and took the reins. They drove back to the village without exchanging another word.

CHAPTER SIX

The following week, during the early morning service in the village church, the door was flung open with a crash which brought all heads swinging round in surprise. A disheveled figure lurched inside, paused, stared round the church, and roared, "Hypocrites! Whited sepulchres . . ."

There was a gasp of shocked amazement. Sabrina saw several of the women draw their skirts closer, as if against contamination. Miss Furness, the blacksmith's daughter, sucked in her breath as her father always did shoeing horses, her church bonnet vibrating visibly.

Louisa held her hymnal to her face and from behind this cover murmured, "It is the Duckett man, the cowman from Sweet Briars . . . how disgusting, he is in liquor . . ." Her lips drew in primly, but her brown eyes had the shine of warm brandy balls as she gazed over her hymnal at the man.

The yawning formality of the usual service evaporated in a bustle of barely repressed excitement. This was something new, something more interesting than the singing of psalms.

The Vicar, who had been in the pulpit, hurriedly descended, gesturing to the sidesmen, but their attention was riveted upon Will Duckett, and they did

103

not notice the Vicar's attempt to catch their eye.

Reeling, Will Duckett advanced into the aisle. His face was pallid, perspiring, his eyes set in a rigid glare.

He caught a pew back and leaned forward to shout at the nearest occupant, the baker, Jack Wallis, a plump, pink, clean man, with thining gray hair and an expression of righteous satisfaction. Wallis drew back, his nostrils pinched, from the other's odor of sweat and beer. "Cheat, hypocrite," Will accused him. "There's no religion in you, what are you doing here? You give short weight with every quartern loaf. Cheat! What does it matter to you that my children will rot in the workhouse for want of a few pence? You have guineas in your pockets and a roast dinner to go home to, don't you?"

"You are drunk, Duckett," Mr. Wallis whispered, hotly conscious of the listening ears, "drunk on a Sunday morning . . . disgusting! Go home and sleep it off, man."

"Oh, aye, I'm drunk! And why not? I'm to be kenneled like a useless old dog, fed scraps and spat upon by hypocrites like you! Workhouse fodder, that's me! And after fifteen years working hard for a man who pays me barely enough to keep body and soul together! There's no justice!"

The village gossips were humming like tops at this delicious scene, committing each word to memory religiously. It was a long time since Ambresbury had had such a scandal.

All eyes turned upon the Links, stiff as boards in their pew, their faces frozen towards the altar. Only little Emily dared to peep behind.

"Will, Will," intoned the Vicar, "this is the house of God . . ."

Will turned on him savagely, "That to God!" he shouted, spitting on the floor of the aisle. "What has he ever done for me?"

"Sacrilege," the congregation murmured to each other, striving to keep their smiles off their faces. "Blasphemy . . . how disgusting . . . so shocking . . . Goodness me . . . Well, I never . . ."

A buzz of voices broke out all over the church as neighbors turned to speak to each other.

The sidesmen had caught Mr. Fraser's eye and now advanced upon Will, squaring their shoulders.

He turned on them. "Come on, then . . . Come on, Joe Higgins, come on, Peter Fowler . . . I'm a match for three of you . . ."

He was a big, thick-set man, in his rage impressive enough to keep them hesitating, each waiting for the others to move first.

"Will, would you brawl in the house of God?" Mr. Fraser pleaded. "Go quietly. We are all very sorry for you, indeed, but to break into our prayers in this way . . ." His tone was dignified, but Sabrina saw that he was very pale and was careful to keep out of Will's reach.

Johnny stood up and walked back down the aisle, past their pew, his face calm and expressionless.

"Keep out of this, Doctor," Will warned. "I've no quarrel withee . . ."

"This is achieving nothing, Will," Johnny said firmly. "Come outside with me and leave them to their prayers. You are only making matters worse for your family. Do you want them to commit you to a constable for a breach of the peace?"

"What do I care?" Will growled sullenly.

Johnny placed his hand on Will's shoulder. "Be sensible, man," he said.

The laborer shook his shoulder, at the same time turning to smash his fist full into Johnny's stomach. Johnny crumpled, his hands at his stomach, groaning, and the sidesmen rushed on Will and bore him down, struggling, fists flying, in a noisy heap of bodies.

Sabrina felt sick, her anxious eyes watching Johnny as he very slowly rose, clutching at a pew to assist him.

"Let him go!" he said angrily, his voice thick with pain, and pulled one of the men off Will.

His voice cut through the fury of their fight. The authority rang out in their ears, and one by one the men stood back, leaving Will, blood pouring from a cut lip, his left eye beginning to swell and discolor, to get to his feet.

Johnny took him by one arm and marched him out of the church. The door banged back behind them, and the congregation sat like stone figures, staring.

Sighing with relief, the Vicar returned to the pulpit, in a flurry of white lace and black cloth, and gave out a hymn. As the quavering voices rose up, Sabrina discreetly slipped out of the Squire's pew, leaving her sister and cousin staring after her, and followed Johnny outside.

She found him walking towards his cottage, Will Duckett half leaning on him.

Johnny frowned at her when she hurried up. "Get back to the church."

She shook her head. "I want to talk to Mr. Duckett."

The laborer looked at her, his expression dazed now, depleted, as if he had used up all his energy and was now in a state of near collapse.

"He is not fit to talk to anyone," Johnny said. "Morbid curiosity cannot help him."

She flushed angrily. "I want to help him in a practical way," she retorted. "I was going to suggest that one of his daughters could be taken into Ambreys to work in the kitchen. Molly says her sister, Nan, is capable, even though she is only nine."

Johnny's lip was twisted in a grimace. "I am sorry," he said brusquely. "Yes, it is a good suggestion. Do you hear, Will? Miss Crammond is going to take one of your children out of the workhouse."

Will Duckett turned bloodshot, miserable eyes on her. "Thankee, Miss," he mumbled.

Johnny pushed open his front door, and Will Duckett stumbled inside. Sabrina went through to the kitchen, which was empty, clean and cold. She found a bottle of rum in a cupboard and poured a large glass which she took through to the parlor where Johnny was forcing the laborer to sit down. Johnny took the glass, stared at it, then at her.

"He has had enough of this," he said.

But Will raised his head, saw the glass and put out a shaking hand. Sighing, Johnny gave him the rum, and Will swallowed it.

His body shuddered convulsively, then he looked up. "Thank you, Miss," he said, in stronger tones.

"I feel better now." He tried to get up, but Johnny put a restraining hand on his shoulder.

"You need your face seen to," he told him kindly.

Sabrina returned to the kitchen, found some clean cloth and a bowl of water, and returned again to the parlor. Johnny gently cleansed Will's injuries.

"When did Link tell you that you had to go?" he asked as he worked.

"Last night," Will said dully. "I went straight out to old Mother Green's ale house."

"And been there all night, by the smell of you," Johnny commented, gently dabbing at the bruised eye. "You'll have quite a shiner here, Will—all colors of the rainbow."

Will shrugged. "What does it matter?"

"Very little," Johnny agreed. "I suppose you don't know anyone who might take you on? No other farmer?"

Will gave him a long look. "They are laying men off, not taking them on. Farming is in a terrible way. All over Essex men are being turned off the farms. I never thought it would happen to me. Fifteen years I've been cowman to Link."

"Hmm . . ." Johnny carefully dried his face with the towel Sabrina offered him. "There you are, then. I can do no more. Nature must heal these on her own." He looked at Sabrina, "Make us some black coffee, will you?"

She went back to the kitchen and made a pot of very strong black coffee. When she carried it through, she heard Johnny saying, "Rob shall come here to me—he could be useful to me. A quick, bright lad.

There's a room over my stable. He can sleep there. I would take some of the others, but I really have no room."

"I want no charity," Will growled, looking hard at him.

"No charity, man—I'll expect him to learn and work. We'll both of us benefit."

"Thank you, Doctor," Will muttered, then dropped his head into his hands. "They shave your heads, you know, in the House. You queue up for your food, like convicts, and little enough of it you get!"

With a bleak face, Johnny touched his shoulder. "I know."

"And they take the women and children off to another part. We won't be together. It isn't allowed! Is that right or natural? A man needs his wife. When we were wed, Parson said . . ." he stopped, shaking his head. "I can't remember the words, but something about whom God hath joined let no man separate. And they are going to, Doctor. Is it right?"

"Drink your coffee, Will," Johnny said grimly.

Will obeyed like a child, his shoulders drooping. Then Johnny offered to drive him home, but he said that he preferred to walk. "The new little one," he said, looking at Johnny, his face quivering with emotion, "the baby we're expecting, what sort of world is it to bring a child into . . . It will be born in the Workhouse hospital. A pauper brat. Taken away from my poor wife and fed on gruel until it is old enough to be sold into slavery. Better for it if it dies first."

Johnny led him to the door and pressed something into his hand as he went. Will pushed it back, half angry, "No, no, thank you, but no."

When he had gone, Johnny came back and sank into his chair with a long heavy sigh. "Do you feel guilty, Sabrina?" he asked without looking up.

"Guilty?" she echoed, puzzled.

"You ought to," he said. "We all ought to, but we do not. We feel charitable giving these devils the sanctuary of the Workhouse. We cannot understand why they object to having their heads shorn, their bodies scrubbed clean, their lives regimented. They have useful work to do, food to eat, a roof over their heads. How ungrateful of them to refuse to be happy!"

"It is nobody's fault," she protested. "Even Mr. Link, unpleasant as he is, cannot help it if he cannot afford to employ all his men anymore."

"Oh, such a useful excuse," Johnny said savagely. "Economic forces! It is the way our world wags, isn't it? And so we have our own permission to shrug it off and enjoy our own lives while people like the Ducketts sink under the burden of their misery."

"Well, what can you do?" she asked, "beg Mr. Link to keep him?"

"Oh, that would set him up with himself for weeks," he said dryly. "Link hates the gentry, didn't you realize it? He is an ambitious man, thwarted by his own circumstances. He feeds his envy and malice by thinking how much more he deserves what your uncle inherited. He regards me with contempt because I choose to live here, earning a pittance, rather than work in London with my uncle. He sees me as a weak and ineffectual idealist, practically a lunatic!"

"Hateful man," she said angrily, "I detest him!"

"Thank you," he said, grinning at her.

She flushed. "Perhaps if you spoke to my uncle?" she suggested after a pause, "he might persuade Link to relent."

"I doubt if it would do much good. You forget, your uncle's income largely depends upon the rents of his farms. And after Will's behavior this morning, I doubt if your uncle will listen." He shrugged, "However, I will try, for the children's sake."

When she arrived back at Ambreys, she was suddenly reminded of her own impulsive and unseemly exit from the church.

Aunt Maria received her in the drawing room, stiff with outrage, and blazed at her for some time. "Totally shameless . . . what the neighbors thought . . . embarrassing Doctor Graham, making him a laughingstock . . . Heaven only knows what he made of your conduct! No young lady could think of such behavior . . . scullery maids would shrink from it . . . Walking out of church in full view of everybody . . . People staring . . . Poor Louisa! Forward and indelicate, Miss! He will despise you for it, you may be sure!"

Since her rage was caused not by Sabrina's public exit from church itself but by jealousy for her daughter's chances of marrying Johnny, she was not to be propitiated by assurances of regret.

"I acted upon impulse," Sabrina pleaded, only to be repulsed.

"I know your impulses, Miss! They always bring

you forward into the spotlight. You must always be noticed!"

"I was sorry for Mr. Duckett's children," Sabrina retorted, angry now herself.

"That man! Drunken brawling in the church! Spitting on the church floor! Scandalous! Oh, a fit object for your charity, Miss, I'm sure!"

"He may have behaved wrongly in church," Sabrina began, only to be interrupted.

"May! May! I have never been so shocked in my life! Poor Mrs. Fraser fainted and had to be carried into the vestry . . ." But Aunt Maria's hatred for the Vicar's wife would not be suppressed even in a moment of stress. Her lips twitched, a smile of positive triumph was quickly controlled. "I was quite sorry for her," she said, with ineffable condescension. "Poor woman, to see her husband insulted in his own church, it was too much!"

Sabrina finally escaped, her ears ringing with denunciations, and went upstairs. She found Charity and Louisa waiting for her, having heard something of the scene in the drawing room, from a vantage point on the stairs.

Charity's quiet sympathy expressed itself in the removal of her outdoor clothes. Untying her bonnet strings, she gently stroked back some stray red hairs, smiling into her sister's eyes with comforting assurance.

Louisa watched, seated on Sabrina's bed, her arms folded, her lips thin and mutinous. When Charity had disposed of Sabrina's bonnet and cloak, Louisa said grimly, "Well, cousin? Where did you go when you ran out of church?"

"I helped Doctor Graham to quiet him," Sabrina said, quite as furious now as either her aunt or her cousin. She knew she had been foolish to act impulsively, but she did not think her behavior warranted such outbursts of wrath as it had received.

Louisa's face flushed. "Oh, indeed?" she said, her eyes protruding.

"Oh, Sabrina, he might have harmed you," Charity murmured, unhappily.

Louisa was very red now, her cheeks shiny and puffy. "No wonder Mama was shouting at you! You deserve every word she said! But you are mistaken if you imagine such cheap tricks will deceive Doctor Graham. He is not the man to be taken in by your snares!"

"Oh, Louisa!" gasped Charity, deeply upset. She stared from one to the other, wringing her hands and shaking her head. "Do not be angry with each other!"

Louisa, however, was looking remarkably like her Mama. Her lips and eyes were narrow slits, her chin very angular. "Men do not like flirts!" she informed Sabrina. "They never marry them. You will only make yourself a laughing stock, running after him in such a fast and vulgar fashion! I am really quite sorry for you! If I were you I should be content with Byrd Johnstone. He is not precisely a gentleman, but he is very wealthy, and you will be fortunate if you can catch him! If he were not a tradesman's son, I might even consider him myself."

"Generous of you," said Sabrina tartly, herself now in a bitter rage.

Louisa sniffed, "I daresay he wishes to be related

to our family, or he would not show you such attentions. He is aware that my Mama could not consider him. His background is not such as we could admit! But for you, he would do very well."

Sabrina dug her nails into her palms. "Thank you!"

Louisa walked to the door, paused, looked round. "But Doctor Graham is a gentleman, and soon to be a wealthy one. His family would not allow him to marry beneath him. He will marry in his own sphere."

Sabrina did not answer, and Louisa went out, closing the door with a bang.

Sabrina pressed her hands to her hot face. She was aware of a dampness in her eyes which soon became a stream of tears down her cheeks.

"Sabrina!" Aghast, Charity crouched beside her. "You are crying! Louisa did not mean it! I have never heard her speak so before! She was wounded because you have been with Doctor Graham. It is a settled thing, you know, that they are to marry when his brother dies! She is so attached to him, you must not mind what she said."

Sabrina grimaced. "I am sorry for his brother. Poor young man, only interesting because he must soon die and leave all he possesses to his brother so that his brother may be fit to marry Louisa!"

"Oh, what a wicked thing to say!" said Charity, drawing back. "Oh, Sabrina, that was not worthy of you! It is not like that!"

"Do you honestly believe that Louisa would marry Johnny if he were poor?" Sabrina demanded fiercely.

Charity went white. "Johnny?" she repeated, in a

shocked tone. "You used his name!" There was a silence, in which they gazed at each other, and then Charity asked, "What does it mean, Sabrina? I have sometimes noticed with what familiarity you speak to each other. There is an intimacy between you that I cannot like."

Sabrina pulled herself together and spoke slowly, with a forced, bright smile. "Your imagination again, Charity! It is Doctor Graham's bedside manner which makes him speak with such easiness to everyone! And as for me, why, I am so prone to speak my mind, you know, I cannot always remember to be formal and polite to everyone!"

"Aunt Maria would never forgive you if you came between Louisa and the Doctor," Charity warned, watching her uneasily.

Sabrina shrugged. "She need not be anxious on that score. I have no claims upon him."

"Louisa is truly attached to him," Charity said, in a half relieved, half nervous voice. "I do not think she would care if he were poor."

Sabrina nodded. "He is very handsome," she said lightly, and felt a strange pleasure in saying aloud what she had often thought secretly. She had often longed to share with her sister all that she felt on this subject. It was a bitter delight to hear Johnny praised, hear his name mentioned, although she could not confess to Charity all that she really felt.

Charity frowned and wove her hands into a tent, nervously, "Sabrina, I hope . . ." She hesitated and did not go on, looking at her sister with wide, anxious eyes.

Sabrina knew very well what she wished to ask,

but she did not choose to understand, and quickly changed the subject by asking Charity some question about the rapidly approaching ball.

At dinner that evening, Aunt Maria regarded her with a smoldering and suspicious gaze, and Louisa, still a little flushed and stiff in her manner, never spoke to her at all.

Uncle Matthew had invited Johnny to dine with them, and over his well heaped plate of veal in wine sauce, informed them that he had agreed to give the Duckett child a trial in the kitchen.

His wife awesomely asked if the hiring of kitchen hands were to be taken out of her dispensation altogether, and Uncle Matthew gave her an irritable glance.

"Do not be ridiculous, my dear. Have you some objection to my plan? The child must otherwise go into the Workhouse."

Aunt Maria informed him that she preferred to choose her own staff. "I am the best judge, after all," she added.

"On most occasions, yes," he retorted, "but in this event, I have made the decision, and you must abide by it." And he would hear no more upon the matter. "I am only sorry I cannot give the father employment, but all my positions are filled, and I know the other tenants are turning men off, too. We are all in the same boat. Farm prices must pick up some time, however. We must all be patient and trust in providence." And he thrust a forkful of veal, dripping in rich sauce, into his mouth, and contentedly chewed.

Aunt Maria and Louisa exchanged glances. Louisa was bright-eyed, thin-lipped.

"Doctor Graham," murmured Aunt Maria, turning towards him with a warm smile, "will you have a little more?"

He shook his head, "No, I thank you. This is delicious, but highly spiced, and I dare eat no more of it or I will not be able to do justice to the rest of the meal."

She beamed. "Then you may clear . . ." glancing at the servants who sprang forward at once.

She leaned forward again, "You know that my son's betrothal is to be announced at Miss Colling's ball, Doctor?"

"I had heard so," he said, smiling, "I felicitate you. She is a very charming girl."

Aunt Maria simpered. "Oh, indeed! We are all very happy." She paused, then said casually, "Of course, you will attend, Doctor."

He smiled. "Thank you, I should be very happy."

"Some of the guests will be from London," she went on, in the same very easy way. "One or two of them are acquainted with your uncle, Sir Lucas Graham, I understand."

He looked up, his face cool, very intent, and Sabrina felt a little shiver of apprehension at this mention of the man who had ruined her happiness. She was deeply conscious of the fact that Johnny did not look at her, although his very manner conveyed his own reaction to be similar to her own.

"My uncle is well known in many circles," he said quietly.

"Oh, indeed," Aunt Maria said graciously, "and as respected, I am sure, as you, Dr. Graham, in our own small world."

He inclined his head. "You are very kind."

"Lady Colling, indeed, has expressed to me a wish that your uncle might be invited to the ball," she went on, more rapidly, her gaze not quite resting on his face, her tone bright and not easy. "We are eager to make you feel at home with us, Doctor, and it would be a great honor to receive your nearest relation here in our midst."

Johnny shot Sabrina a quick glance, his expression unreadable. She had gone white. She felt the hairs on the back of her neck standing up. Her hands trembled as she pushed her plate away, the remains of her pudding unfinished.

"You are most gracious," he said, very very slowly. "And, please believe me, I am deeply grateful for such a kind thought. But, this is a family occasion, a time when you will wish to enjoy your happiness alone. My uncle and aunt, being strangers to you, must be out of place at such a party."

"No, no, Doctor," Aunt Maria beamed at him. "Sir Lucas Graham is not unknown to any of us who have friends in London. His name is a famous one, indeed. And we want you to feel at home with us, you know, we want you to feel that you belong to our little circle. You must often feel the wish to see your own family, and here is the perfect opportunity. Lady Colling can put them up, you know!" With a little preening gesture, "The Grange is so spacious!"

Johnny looked down at his plate, his brow troubled. Then he looked up and smiled. "You are too kind, Mrs. Wilton."

Sabrina, who had been listening with the most

painful anxiety, was dismayed. Surely he could not mean to let this happen? The moment Sir Lucas set eyes on her, the cat would be out of the bag. His wife would take great pleasure in exposing her, however public the occasion.

Aunt Maria smiled triumphantly upon Johnny. "Then that is settled," she said, exchanging a glance with Louisa, who looked sideways at Sabrina, tossing her head with an insolent little smile.

Sabrina met the look, forcing herself to appear indifferent, even smiling faintly, although her lips moved so stiffly that she was almost sure they hurt.

When she went up to her room later, she found that her lower lip was torn, the flesh rent and slightly red with blood, where, without knowing it, she had bitten through. She sat down and slowly brushed her hair. The gentle motion eased her physically, made the dull ache of her heart less painful, but her mind was in constant turmoil.

Somehow, she thought, she must avoid appearing at Charlotte's ball, so that she might avoid meeting Sir Lucas again. But how? What excuse could she possibly give?

And, what of Johnny? Why had he given in to her aunt's demand? Did he mean to allow her to be exposed? She had imagined, at first, that he was concerned and meant to oppose the idea, and then, after a glance at Louisa, he had given in to her aunt.

Was he seriously pursuing Louisa, then? She was clearly serious in her hopes of him, and, of course, it must be admitted that it would be a good match. Louisa would have a private income of some weight. Her family was good, her reputation unblemished.

She was not beautiful, even pretty, but if men only married for beauty, the world would be full of unmarried women. Sabrina could not be certain, but she suspected that Johnny was, indeed, thinking of marriage. He was uncomfortable in his cottage and often complained of being neglected by his servant. When he succeeded to his brother's estate, he must need a wife, to provide heirs. Why not, then, Louisa, who so obviously encouraged him and was so very suitable?

On the following day, Byrd Johnstone visited them to discuss his plans for a picnic on his grounds. He had stopped in the village for Johnny, and the two young men were loudly welcomed by Louisa and her mother when they arrived. Johnny did not look at Sabrina, seated in a corner of the quiet morning room, sewing one of the gifts she was making for Charlotte, a cambric shift of delicate workmanship and exquisite embroidery.

Byrd, however, came to her and sat down, saying that it seemed a very long time since they last met.

Only too conscious of Louisa chattering to Johnny who sat beside her at the table, endeavoring to guess a riddle she had been teasing Charity with earlier, Sabrina answered with more warmth than she would otherwise have used and was ashamed to see Byrd's face light up with pleasure.

Louisa looked round once or twice and made some comment to Johnny, laughing, clearly pointing out to him Byrd's close attendance upon her cousin. Sabrina, although aware of it, tried to seem unconscious of anything but her companion, and listened attentively to all he said. Her eyes and ears, although apparently set upon him only, were in reality closely following the events on the other side of the room.

She saw Louisa's happy smiles, saw her aunt beam upon the two, heard Johnny's voice, deep, slow and pleasant, as he made some reply to one of Louisa's questions.

"So you open the village school in the autumn?" Byrd asked her.

"Yes, and we are well advanced with all our preparations," she said. "I have drawn up a syllabus which I believe will suit, and my house is fit to be occupied at any moment. I eagerly look forward to the day when I may see my plans put into operation."

He looked seriously at her. "It still seems strange to me, and I cannot believe you suitable for so demanding a position. A young woman of lesser birth and smaller means must be more apt. You have been brought up too delicately for it."

She laughed, thinking of her strict childhood, the long hours of study, the frugal means and the plain clothes. "You are very wrong," she said, shaking her head; "I am most apt, I assure you."

He lowered his voice, fixing his eyes upon her with the utmost absorption. "You would be better fitted to be the wife of some fortunate fellow." Then he halted, looking flushed and uncertain, and she read in his face an indecision which she understood. She knew, by now, that Byrd admired her, that the thought had passed through his mind that she would make an excellent wife, but that her lack of fortune must be a barrier.

Calmly she lowered her eyes and resumed her sewing. "I am perfectly happy as I am," she said quietly, and felt his relief warring with his admiration.

But he drew back again, and their talk passed on to less personal matters. And Sabrina was glad of it because she knew that she could never return his affection adequately. Her own affections were too securely given elsewhere.

Byrd raised the matter of his proposed picnic to the whole assembled company and had it greeted with delight by Aunt Maria and Louisa.

"Charming idea. Just what is needed to bridge the gap between spring and full summer. A picnic is so refreshing," Aunt Maria said.

"You'll come, Graham?" Byrd said cheerfully, and Johnny agreed without hesitation.

"If I am not wanted elsewhere," he added.

"You shall not be," Louisa promised. "We will threaten anyone who dares to be ill on that day with the most awful punishments!"

Sabrina, looking at her, saw that her discontented, sullen look had given way to a sort of easy confidence. Charity had done her work well, and was now well nigh discarded. Louisa barely spoke to her, devoting herself entirely to Johnny, hanging on every word, every look, with a bright smile of approval and interest.

Charity, seated apart from them, might have been entirely elsewhere, for all the notice taken of her. She was looking pale and wistful, Sabrina noted, her mouth drooping a little, her eyes cast down.

Byrd saw where Sabrina's eyes rested, and said, "Is your sister not well?"

"She looks a little neglected," Sabrina whispered, and aloud, "Charity, come here a moment. We wish to ask you something!"

The little group around the table looked up at that and stared. Charity, flushing at the sudden summons, rose and came willingly, taking the seat Byrd drew up for her, with a shy smile.

"We are discussing whether to have the picnic near the house, for fear of sudden shower, or down by the river, under the trees, where it will be most pleasant, if it is a warm day."

Charity considered seriously. "Oh, let us risk a storm," she said eagerly, "down by the river. That is far the best."

Byrd laughed. "My views entirely, Miss Charity. There is a spot there which has the best view of any in the county."

"What are you saying?" Louisa asked curiously, and was informed of their decision in which she thoroughly concurred.

"Oh, but the midges," cried Aunt Maria, "under trees, beside a river. Mr. Johnstone, there are certain to be midges, and it will be fatal for Louisa to be bitten by insects just before the great ball."

"If an insect bites Miss Louisa," Byrd returned calmly, with a twinkling eye, "I shall smite the daring insect, hip and thigh."

Aunt Maria was not sure how to take this, and looked both shocked and coy at once. "Mr. Johnstone," she protested faintly.

He smiled. "Do not be afraid, Mrs. Wilton. There will be no shortage of gentlemen ready to protect

Miss Louisa's complexion against all the ravages of midges, wasps, ants and dragonflies."

"Dragonflies!" giggled Louisa. "Oh, Mama, he is teasing you!"

Aunt Maria allowed herself to laugh. "Such a wicked tease," she murmured uncertainly.

When the gentlemen got up to leave, Byrd kissed Sabrina's hand. "I look forward to showing you my home," he said softly.

Conscious of her aunt's interested, not unapproving gaze, she flushed and murmured some incoherent reply which seemed to satisfy him.

"I wrote to your uncle today, Doctor," Aunt Maria said, as they stood on the portico to see the gentlemen ride away. "I have invited him, as promised, and I hope he will spend the week here, as our guest."

Johnny looked up sharply. "Very kind," he murmured, "very thoughtful," and his glance slid smoothly over Sabrina.

She tensed, her hands clenching at her side, and wondered that no one seemed to notice the physical shock the news had given her. Her own heart seemed to beat so loudly it must surely be audible to them all, and she felt the blood running from her face, leaving her white and icy.

"Has the letter gone?" Johnny asked. "I have not written to my uncle for some weeks, and I should have been glad to add a few lines imploring him to make every effort to attend."

Aunt Maria cried, "Why, that is an excellent idea! Louisa, fetch the letter from my writing bureau.

It is not yet sealed down. Have you time to write a few lines now, Doctor?"

"Why do I not take it with me and post it for you?" he said smoothly. "I will be at my leisure then, to persuade him by all in my powers, to accept your kind invitation. He is so busy, you know, that he rarely leaves London. The Family require constant attendance."

This reference to the Royal Family so excited Aunt Maria that had he asked her to cut off her head and serve it for supper, she would have been sorely tempted to comply. She took the letter which Louisa brought out and handed it down to Johnny with a broad smile of encouragement.

"Now, be sure to say all you can to bring him to us," she said.

Johnny thrust the letter into his jacket. "I shall," he said seriously. "Be certain of that!"

Sabrina watched the two men ride away down the drive. Her body trembled convulsively, and her eyes were dilated in shock. Johnny was about to betray her. She had only two clear weeks before the ball, and then she would be brought face to face with the two people in the world whom she least wished to see again.

That would be bad enough, but to think that it was Johnny who was making it possible, Johnny who was deliberately bringing this upon her head! The thought was unbearable. How he must hate her to do this! She could only imagine that he had determined to marry Louisa and was removing her from the scene before Louisa discovered their past involvement.

She watched her cousin walk back into the house, and felt fierce hatred. Louisa, then, was to be Johnny's wife! And she was to be once more dismissed in shame for something she had not done. The injustice of it burned in her chest.

CHAPTER SEVEN

Next morning Charity sat with Sabrina in the morning room, reading from a work of devotion, but her eyes now and then rising to look seriously at her sister. They were alone for once, and, becoming aware of these glances, Sabrina asked, "What is it?"

Charity seemed disturbed by this direct question, but after a moment asked hesitantly, "Was not your employer while you were in London called Graham?"

Sabrina had been wondering when the realization would strike. Charity had been far more interested in London itself than in her sister's employers, and clearly had forgotten their name, but soon or later, Sabrina had expected the memory to return. It was fortunate that Charity's discretion had led her to await a private moment for her questions.

"Yes," she said calmly. She deliberately made her tone as unrevealing as she could, trusting to Charity's delicacy of mind to restrain her from too many questions. She knew her sister would notice her tone and draw her own conclusions.

She was justified. Charity looked very seriously at her. "Oh? Indeed? And related to Sir Lucas, perhaps?"

Sabrina said quietly that it had been Sir Lucas himself.

Charity showed no sign of surprise. She nodded, glancing down at her book again. There was a pause of some moments before she spoke again.

"You do not wish to discuss the subject, Sabrina?"

"No," Sabrina agreed quietly, "I would rather not do so—and, please, Charity, do not mention this to anyone, will you?"

"Of course, if you do not wish it, I will forget the whole matter," Charity said, frowning, but Sabrina was very conscious of the deep thoughtfulness of her manner and her frequent glances in her direction.

It was not possible, of course, even with Charity, for a certain curiosity to remain hidden. Human nature prompted the birth of a new train of ideas. Sabrina could read them in her sister's face. Sabrina's own nature, impulsive, direct, vigorous, must be oddly at variance with her request for silence on the subject of her time in London. Charity had hitherto put this down to a dislike of being in a position of inferiority among strangers, but now that she had connected Sabrina's doubtful intimacy, as she saw it, with John Graham, she must be linking all the other strange actions: her sister's scanty, unrevealing letters from London, her sudden unexplained return, her subsequent silence. What she thought she did not say, but her face was troubled and uneasy.

Tom came home two days later, his features brown from exposure to the elements, talking excitedly of the beauties of Scotland, and of the sport he had had with his cousin.

Uncle Matthew, delighted to have masculine company in the house once more, bore him off to the stables to see a new hunter which he had that week purchased for Tom's exclusive use, and kept him from the ladies for hours, so interested was he in all he heard of his son's experiences.

Aunt Maria was contented enough at this, being still eager to keep Tom away from his attractive cousin, but at dinner her delight in her son overflowed enough for her to turn a blind eye to his occasional compliment to Sabrina.

His experiences in Scotland had improved him, indeed, giving him the slightest gloss of maturity, a pleasant polish to his manners, so that he no longer pursued Sabrina with such eagerness. He did show a tendency to boast of a supposed conquest, a young lady met in Scotland who he had imagined showed a preference for him, but he had improved enough to talk light-heartedly of it, and was ready to laugh at himself over it.

The beginning and end of his enthusiasm, however, was his cousin, a regular sportsman, he informed them repeatedly, who fished, shot, hunted with amazing dexterity. This cousin, older than himself, had, it became clear, made fun of Tom's romantic tendencies, and this Tom had taken to heart.

"Jamie says that Charlotte sounds like a very sensible girl," he informed them, stuffing broiled trout into his mouth without pause. "Jamie intends to look out for just such a wife. He says most girls are too silly to marry. What one should look for, in his opinion, is a girl who can sit a horse well and does not jump at the sound of a shotgun."

Jamie, it appeared, was now invited to the betrothal ball, and looked forward to meeting Charlotte. "And I am sure she will like him," Tom said complacently. "I think I will ride over tomorrow and let her see my new hunter. She is a good judge of horseflesh, for a girl."

Sabrina spent a great deal of her time over the next few days in the School House, although, in fact, she had so well prepared for the opening of the school that she had little to do. But the atmosphere at Ambreys was no longer pleasant for her. Her cousin, Louisa, was sullenly hostile, her aunt ungenerous. All that she achieved by remaining within reach of their unkindness was to disturb Charity, upon whom fell the burden of maintaining a polite conversation when most of the participants were icily withdrawn.

When she was not present, Sabrina suspected, Louisa and Charity still got on well enough, for Charity would not argue with her cousin, and Louisa was not disposed to quarrel with the one person whom she could shine down both in appearance and conversation. For the moment, Charity was useful to Louisa, and Sabrina could know that she helped her sister by staying away all day.

Uncle Matthew, when they met, was as indifferently kind as ever, happy, so long as he had his horses and dogs to escape to, never wishing to involve himself with domestic affairs unless his own sense of responsibility unavoidably forced this upon him. Now and then, when they met alone, he would look at her a little wistfully, and say, "How like your mother you are, my dear! We were very close, once!" And she felt that because of this likeness she was an object of interest to him, in a way Charity was not, a visible link with his childhood, of which he was fond, although his moral laziness made him disguise the fact before his wife.

The day of Byrd's picnic dawned bright and clear. The family were up early to breakfast together before setting out at a little after nine for Byrd's farm.

They drove in the carriage, with Tom riding alongside, galloping ahead from time to time in great high spirits, to come back with a shout and a hallo, calling out to them some remark as to the weather or the scenery.

They paused in Ambresbury to wait for Johnny, who was to ride with Tom, and then made more speed along the quiet lanes, with the two young men racing each other from landmark to landmark.

For Sabrina the sight of Johnny was quiet misery. She could hardly bear to look at him. Every morning she had awaited the arrival of the post with tense anxiety, expecting the letter from London which would herald her doom, but so far there had been no answer from Sir Lucas to the invitation.

Louisa's emotions were more openly displayed. She hung from the window, watching Johnny with excited admiration, describing to them his progress in gasps and hyperbole, "Oh, he has leapt a fence . . . Mama, Mama, indeed, I never saw such a leap . . . His horsemanship is superb . . . Oh, he is coming back . . . Doctor Graham, Doctor Graham, do not ride so fast, you will break your neck. He has not heard me, he is coming at such a gallop . . ."

"Take care, Miss Louisa, you will get a speck of dust in your eye, hanging out like that," was his comment as he paused by the window.

"Then you would have to take it out," she sighed, smiling at him from behind her hand.

He looked as if he did not know quite how to take such an invitation, but laughed. "Better not to get it there at all," he said, turning his mount to ride off.

They made good time, and as they drove up towards Byrd's elegant little house found him waiting for them, watch in hand, exclaiming at their early arrival. "This is very good! I had not hoped to see you for another half hour at least. Come in, come in, my housekeeper has refreshments laid out in the drawing room, and you must all be parched with thirst after such a long, dusty ride."

His housekeeper waited upon them as they went in and showed by her smiles and courtesy her pleasure in this rare piece of hospitality.

"Mrs. Goudge is forever complaining that we have no visitors from among my friends," he said, laughing. "All my visitors are farmers come to inspect the farm, and she finds them dull company to entertain, for they rarely bring their wives, you know, and a woman must always judge her own standards of housekeeping by the reactions of other women."

Mrs. Goudge looked at him with indulgent contempt but said nothing to dispute his assertions.

"You malign our sex," Aunt Maria said coyly. "I am sure that Mrs. Goudge means no such thing."

He looked at Sabrina, inviting her to speak, but she only smiled and shook her head.

The housekeeper looked sharply at her then, and glanced at her master as if making a sudden deduction, and Sabrina saw him catch that glance, and smile, half sheepish, half pleased.

After they had refreshed themselves, they went out to see the farm. The party divided itself naturally into two groups. Byrd walked ahead with Sabrina, Johnny and Louisa, and Aunt Maria followed on with Tom and Charity, perfectly contented to walk at a slower pace while her son was with her, more interested in hearing him talk of Charlotte's favorable opinion of his new hunter than in the disposition of Byrd's farm.

Byrd talked easily and with authority of his experiments, and was obviously most proud of his fine fat cattle, a breed he had himself improved by careful selection and breeding over some years.

He spoke of them with the same fond pride as a father talks of his sons, and looked eagerly to Sabrina for a similar reaction.

She was suitably enthusiastic, always conscious of Johnny's watching eyes, determined to seem happy even though she was not, and, without herself realizing it, so relieved to feel herself kindly regarded, that she turned to him as a flower turns to the sun.

She stumbled over a hillock, and he took her arm and helped her along, retaining her arm afterwards as if unaware. Warmed by his attentions, she leaned on his hand and smiled when their eyes met.

The sun rose higher as the morning progressed, the lazy midges circled under the trees, and the grass was dry and warm against her hand when she brushed it over the banks. There were no men in the fields. Everything lay sleepy, open and fertile, the many shades of green running into each other, rolling fields stretching on either side under hay or wheat or pasture for Byrd's cattle. The hedges were constantly erupting with song as chaffinches, blackbirds, tits, flew in and out. Elms and oaks dotted the landscape, giving balance to the view. The sky was clear and blue, and there was no wind.

"Oh, it is so beautiful," she said softly,. as Byrd helped her over a stile, and he looked up at her with a look almost of gratitude.

"I am glad you like it," he said with enthusiasm, and she saw that he had misunderstood her, and imagined her to be referring to the farm rather than to the day and the countryside around them.

She allowed him to remain in ignorance.

They came down to the spot he had chosen for the picnic as his housekeeper and two servants finished laying the food upon the trestle table set there for the purpose earlier.

Aunt Maria congratulated Mrs. Goudge with stately patronage upon the meal.

"I hope that you enjoy it, Ma'am," the housekeeper murmured, curtseying, but her eyes strayed to Sabrina, at that moment being seated by Byrd upon a soft green cushion of grass under a drooping willow.

"From here you have a fine view of the house," he told her, pointing it out.

She admired the view with sincerity. Set upon a rolling bank, framed between irregular groups of trees, the house looked to advantage from this point, and this had, she suspected, been so planned by someone.

Byrd dismissed the servants, and the men served the ladies before serving themselves, sprawling comfortably by the side of those whom they waited upon when all had full plates.

There was cold game pie, cold fowl, cheese, fruit, pastries. The fresh air gave them an appetite, and the exercise assisted it, so that they made a good meal. Afterwards, they lay in the shade, flushed, replete and idle, talking quietly, none of them willing to make the effort of rising.

The afternoon grew very hot. Drowsy from their meal, they were content enough to enjoy the silence, the cool of the trees, the gentle rippling of the river.

Tom made the first move. He got up impatiently, said, "I think I will stroll along the river! Mama, why do you not come?"

Aunt Maria was happy to oblige him, although her slow rising seemed to say that she, too, would have preferred to continue in her sloth.

Charity wandered away next, to pick buttercups and make bright chains with which to deck herself. Louisa rather fretfully murmured that she wondered what Tom had found so engrossing up by the turn of the river, and looked to Johnny, as if inviting him to suggest joining her brother.

Johnny looked across at Byrd and Sabrina, still lying back in idleness, and said, "Why do we not all walk up there and see?"

"We are happy enough as we are, are we not, Miss Sabrina?" Byrd answered. "But you must go, Graham. Miss Louisa is weary of us. She is eager to expend her energies."

Johnny stood up in a sudden movement, with a violence which made Sabrina jump. "As you please!" he said sharply.

He and Louisa strolled away, talking, but Sabrina saw from the set of his shoulders that Johnny was annoyed over something or other, and the tone of his voice emphasized this displeasure. She wondered what had made him cross. He had been in a reserved mood all day.

Byrd sat up and leaned against the willow, looking down at her vivid face against the grass. "Miss Sabrina," he said suddenly, "I am glad you like my farm. I had hoped you would do so . . ."

His tone and manner sent an alarm up her spine. She felt uneasily that he was again upon the verge of making a declaration. She had no time to consider whether her previous reaction still held good. He had, it seemed, made up his mind, and was now determined to speak.

"We have seen a great deal of each other since you came to Ambreys," he said rapidly. "I have come increasingly to admire and respect you in that time. I am not conceited enough to imagine that your feelings might match my own but will you give me permission to speak to your uncle and seek his approval of a closer relationship?"

His formality made her reply easier. Looking up quickly at him, she saw a kindness in his face that made her believe this deliberate on his part. He had used no words of love, no violence of the emotions which might embarrass or disturb her. She was grateful to him for the way in which he had spoken, and her voice reflected this warmth.

"I am very grateful to you, Byrd," she stammered. "You must know that I have no income to speak of . . ."

He made a gesture of dismissal. "If I wished to marry for money I would have chosen differently," he said. "You have qualities of mind and character that make such issues irrelevant."

She flushed. "Thank you. Will you be offended if I ask for time to consider the question? I had not expected . . . I cannot answer directly . . ."

He reached over and gently touched her hand. "I would think less of you if you answered without due thought. It is a serious question and deserves a serious answer. Please, take all the time you need. I am happy to wait. I think we could be happy together. We share many interests, and I believe we have both enjoyed the time we have spent in each other's company on our rides. I would have spoken earlier. I have not done so now without much thought. But I, too, wished to be sure."

She remembered how he had almost asked her on the day he rode over to Ambreys to protest about her decision to become the village schoolmistress. That had been a generous impulse, and even though he had been clearly reluctant to commit himself at that time, she had known of it, and had been grateful.

She smiled at him. "I am honored that you have asked me. Even if my answer is not the one you want, I shall always remember that you asked."

He looked closely at her. "You are a very beautiful girl, Sabrina," he said, and came closer at that moment to showing emotion than he had when he proposed.

Johnny and Louisa returned at that moment, and clearly had overheard his last remark, for both looked sourly at them and seemed discontented with their stroll.

"Tom has found a dead frog," Louisa said crossly, "and is trying to turn it over with a stick. It made me feel quite sick."

Byrd offered her a sight of a blackbird's nest which he had discovered. "There are three fledglings," he said. "If you push a twig over the nest, they will gape for it. It is a charming sight."

She allowed him to take her along to the bush he indicated and could be heard cooing over the fledglings for a moment, until Byrd strolled off with her to show her some very fine bulrushes.

Sabrina lay, gazing up at the clear sky through the green willow, very much aware of Johnny's silent presence brooding a few feet away from her.

He sat down and put his chin on his knees, gazing at her in silence. "Give me three guesses," he said at last, and she turned her head to look at him in surprise and bewilderment. "As to what Byrd was saying to you," he explained dryly.

She felt herself flush. "Why should you be interested?" she returned defensively.

"Curiosity," he said lightly. He waited a moment, then said, "He was asking you to marry him?"

She sat up, staring down at the river in silence, then said, "Why should you imagine so?"

"It was not my imagination," he said, almost violently, then seemed to regret his manner of speaking and added more coolly, "Well? Am I not right?"

"Surely if you are it is a private matter between myself and Byrd," she said.

He laughed shortly, "Oh, I am right! I have seen

it coming for weeks. Whenever we meet, he talks of nothing but you. The whole district has foreseen it. He is a popular figure. The matchmakers have been busy on his behalf for some years now, with little success. Once or twice they had believed him caught, but nothing has come of it. It is quite a settled thing, now, though. You are to be Mrs. Johnstone before the summer is out."

"How kind of everyone," she said, in irritation. His way of speaking had angered her. She bent her head and stared at the grass. Was it nothing to him, then? He spoke so lightly and carelessly. The indifference of his tone hurt too much for her to be capable of speech for a moment or two.

He, too, seemed averse to speech. He picked a blade of grass and chewed it thoughtfully, threw a pebble down into the water, watched the spreading ripples and then said, "By the way, you may have been anxious about the letter your aunt wrote to my uncle?"

The light voice in which he mentioned what had been an agony of apprehension to her, heaped coals upon her anger. Bitterly, she said, "Oh, no, why should I?"

He ignored her answer. "You need not be," he went on. "I took the liberty of adding a few lines which will certainly keep my uncle away from the ball. Of all things in the world, he most dislikes people who try for free medical advice, and I led him to suppose your aunt to be the worst sort of hypochondriac, eager to have his attendance without having to pay for it. Unless he is very much changed, he will not come."

She was too relieved to speak for a moment. Shame at what she had believed of him, delight that her foreseen humiliation would not happen, so filled her heart that she was forced to be silent or break into foolish tears. She leaned down and picked a daisy, tortured its petals into strange shapes, letting them float away on the sluggish waters among the rustling reeds. When she looked up, he was gazing out over the river with a set face.

"Thank you," she whispered.

He looked round, his features stern. "Now you may accept or refuse Johnstone's proposal without fear," he said coolly.

Byrd and Louisa came back and found them sitting silently watching the river, a few feet apart. Of the little scene which had passed, the only evidence was the few white twisted petals scattered around beside Sabrina.

They walked back to the house and had tea before they left for Ambreys.

Tom was in tearing spirits. He amused himself in teasing his sister, tormenting a spaniel which came padding to greet them and was at once seized by Tom and roughly tickled, and making his mother's head ache, so she claimed, with his noise and foolish humor.

"You have a touch of the sun, Mama," he retorted, "and you ate too much of Byrd's game pies."

The truth of this remark did not soften her. She climbed back into the carriage, clasping her head, moaning. For once her joy in her son was in abatement. She was relieved to see him trot away beside Johnny, and she sat in a corner of the carriage without speaking for the journey, her hand to her head. She was pale enough for her illness to be real. And Louisa's cross humor went unnoticed by her in her own absorption with herself.

That Louisa was very cross was soon apparent. She looked sullenly at Sabrina from time to time, her brown eyes hostile, and was silent as her mother.

For her part, Sabrina was too engrossed with her own thoughts to care what the others were thinking. She could not decide whether to be happy for Johnny's thought and care for her, his chivalry in averting his uncle's threatened visit, or to be miserable because he cared so little that she might marry someone else.

On the whole, she decided to be happy. Happiness had been in short supply for her of late, and she was eager to taste it again. She allowed herself to dwell with delightful folly on Johnny's sternly handsome features, the flash of his dark blue eyes when he spoke violently to her, the curve of his mouth when he smiled, his strength and his gentleness.

It was idiotic, she allowed, but she rationed herself to a brief taste of joy. There was nothing to talk of, nothing to look at, as they moved along the deserted, darkening lanes. She might as well drift into daydreams for that short space of time between leaving Byrd's farm and arriving home.

But the time was more brief than she had expected, for as they rode past the hedges of Sweet Briars Farm, they saw a cart trundling out of a gateway, crowded with weeping children. Sabrina heard Johnny's voice outside the carriage and leaned out to listen.

He was speaking to Mrs. Duckett, seated beside the wagoner, and she heard only snatches of what was said.

"What is it? What is happening?" demanded Louisa, elbowing her out of the way to reach the window.

Johnny turned his mount round and rode up to the window. He looked at Sabrina and spoke only to her, his face intent and angry. "The Ducketts have been evicted," he said tensely. "They are on their way to the Workhouse now. There was some sort of quarrel between Will Duckett and Mr. Link this afternoon. Will lost his temper and struck the fellow, and Link apparently turned them off there and then, threatening to have Will put in jail for it."

"Oh, poor woman," Sabrina said involuntarily.

"That man," snapped Aunt Maria furiously, "that dreadful man! A perfect monster! Drunkard . . ."

"He had not been drinking, Ma'am," Johnny said curtly. "He was beside himself with misery, more like . . ."

"And we pay rates to keep men like him in idleness and luxury," Aunt Maria complained.

"Have they taken him to prison?" Sabrina asked anxiously. "I did not see him on the cart."

Johnny shook his head. "He ran off. He had a shotgun with him, it seems, and is in an angry mood. Mrs. Duckett is afraid of what he may do. Some men are out looking for him now."

"Oh," screamed Aunt Maria, "oh, mercy on us! We are all in danger . . . a madman with a gun . . . it is terrible that such things should be allowed to happen."

"It is," Johnny agreed sardonically, with a glance of utter contempt, and Sabrina could only marvel that her aunt did not see with what scorn he regarded her.

She, however, appeared to see only what she wished to see. "Drive on," she shouted, banging on the side of the carriage. "Whip up the horses . . . The madman may be lurking here with his gun pointed at us . . ."

And the carriage lurched forward suddenly and galloped away towards Ambreys.

CHAPTER EIGHT

No sign was discovered of Will Duckett in the next few days. The search went on, during daylight hours, for forty-eight hours, and then was called off. The general opinion was that the man had either done away with himself and was lying dead somewhere in the forest or had run off to London where he might sink unnoticed into the squalor of the London slums. Little pity was paraded for him. His violent outburst in church had alienated the respectable and amazed the poorer inhabitants. Sabrina burned with anger as she listened to her aunt upon this subject, but she knew better than to speak in his defense. Anything she said would only make her aunt harden her opinion.

Uncle Matthew alone was more tolerant. "It is hard, very hard," he sighed, but he resigned himself without difficulty to a hardship which did not touch himself. "These things happen in the best regulated world!" He congratulated himself on his kindness in taking one of the Duckett children into service in his kitchens and gave orders that she was to be kindly treated, without ever taking any steps to see that his order was obeyed. Sabrina, who did venture down to the kitchens for this purpose, disguising her visit by a desire to pay the cook a compliment upon her

excellent meringue tart, was able to observe that
Nan Duckett was, indeed, treated no better and no
worse than any other servant, and, being quick and
willing, was to some measure approved by the cook.

The arrival of Sir Lucas's letter, politely refusing
Aunt Maria's invitation, lifted Sabrina's spirits
towards the end of the week. Aunt Maria was disap-
pointed but pleased with the stately formality of his
letter, and, as her invitation had been largely a
desire to draw Johnny closer into their circle, could
bear the non-arrival of his uncle with equanimity,
being still hopeful that Johnny was interested in
Louisa.

Uncle Matthew, at breakfast one morning a week
before the ball, observed that it would be a good
thing if his two nieces were now considered to be out
of mourning. "Black is a sad color to be wearing to
a betrothal ball!"

Aunt Maria hurriedly opposed this suggestion on
the grounds of propriety, but her husband, having
thought of this entirely without aid, was stubborn in
pursuit of it.

"Nonsense, it cannot be thought wrong for them
to wear white or lavender. White, perhaps, would be
preferable. It would cast a gloom for them to be
wearing black." And he rose, shrugging off her
further arguments. "There is plenty of time for gowns
to be run up, my dear. I wish to see them both in
some other color than black."

As he then retreated to the stables, Aunt Maria
was forced to concede the point. Irritably, she ordered both Charity and Sabrina to wait indoors for
the dressmaker who was then just finished with

Louisa's new gowns. "Heaven knows if she will be able to do it in time!" she complained.

The gowns they ordered were simple, well cut, in a handsome white silk, the tight sleeves richly embroidered with black, the necklines cut fashionably low, the bodice shaped to their bodies, with full, flouncing skirts and many petticoats. The dressmaker took her cue from her employer and was barely polite, but she was skilled, and the gowns, when they were delivered on the morning of the ball, were more than satisfactory.

Since they were to stay at Colling Grange, the gowns were packed in tissue and loaded on top of the carriage before they set out. Even Louisa was so excited as they drew away from Ambreys that she forgot to show Sabrina her customary hostility and smiled and chattered all the way.

They arrived in the early afternoon and ate a late luncheon with the family. Tom had been staying in the house for two days and was quite at home there, his manner towards his future mother-in-law showing clearly how far his relationship with them had advanced since his return from Scotland.

One of the house guests was his cousin, Jamie, a tall, lean young man of few words, and those very much to the point, whose black hair shone like polished leather.

They strolled in the gardens after lunch. Jamie walked with Sabrina and responded briefly to the various attempts she made at a polite conversation. "Too much cover in the forest," was his only response to her remarks about Epping Forest. And when she spoke of Charlotte, he agreed that she was a pleasant girl. "And has a good seat!"

Tom joined them to tell his cousin of Sabrina's famous escapade with the runaway pony and trap, and then Jamie did look at her with some faint interest.

"Very brave of you," he commented.

Aunt Maria fussed up, "Tom, Charlotte wishes to walk around the rose garden. You must not neglect her today, you know . . ." Her black eyes were darting at Sabrina.

Tom cheerfully returned to his betrothed, and his mother smiled at Jamie. "Cousin, we are very happy to see you down south at last. What do you make of us all, I wonder?"

"I have been south before, you know," he returned. "I was at school here."

"Of course," she said, "when you were at Eton! But you were never in Essex before, I think. It must seem very flat to you after Scotland."

His glance was acute. "Scotland is not all mountains, Aunt," he said.

She laughed. "No, I am sure it is not, but you must call me Cousin Maria, for, you know, I am not your aunt. Your mother is my aunt."

He bowed. "I am sorry, Cousin Maria." But his look was one of dry humor, as if the notion of calling her cousin, with such a discrepancy in their ages, amused him.

Colling Grange was a very large house, rambling and irregular in design, lacking the cohesion of Ambreys which had the beauty of nice proportions to offset the squareness of its design.

They all walked round to the stables later, and Louisa made an outcry when one of the horses, excited by so many strange visitors, kicked out at its stable door, whinnying loudly.

Jamie gave her a look of utter contempt. Charlotte calmly spoke to the frightened animal, walking into the stall without fear to comfort and pet it.

Jamie said to Tom, "That is a very sensible girl, Tom. You will have no trouble with your children learning to ride. I wish I could find a girl with such a spirit."

Spitefully, Louisa said, "Sabrina would suit you, then, Cousin Jamie, for she is afraid of nothing. Even the ordinary conventions of respectable life have no importance for her." And went on to criticize Sabrina for becoming schoolmistress of Ambreys. "Papa has been mortified, I assure you!"

Jamie's slow voice answered, "My mother teaches the children of our crofters, Cousin Louisa. She insists that they all learn to read and write a little, and gives up two days a week to the task. She regards it as her Christian duty."

Louisa was deeply affronted. Very red and thin-lipped, she tossed her head. "Things may be done in Scotland that would not do in England, I assure you, cousin."

Jamie's thin face stiffened. He turned away without replying, but Sabrina saw that his eyes were stormy with insulted pride. She had already discovered his deep sense of national pride and saw that Louisa had made an enemy of him in attacking his country.

The girls went up to rest on their beds for some hours before dressing. Charity and Sabrina had been given a room to share, and they were too excited to sleep, so they lay down and talked softly, in their petticoats, discussing the other guests, particularly Jamie whom Charity thought extremely handsome.

"He reminds me of Papa," she added thoughtfully.

Sabrina laughed. "That stern, unbending air, yes. I think you have hit upon it! I was wondering whom he reminded me of, and this is the answer. He has just Papa's attitude toward females, too. It would freeze my blood to be always in his company."

Charity was shocked and wounded. "How can you say so? Poor, dear Papa, always so certain in his judgment, so moral and good. I am surprised at you, Sabrina."

Sabrina turned her head to stare at her and saw by her look that she was sincere. Was it a yielding desire for some stronger authority which had made Charity her father's victim, then? A yearning for the protection of a powerful masculinity? So that the mental cruelties inflicted by Papa had been borne with resignation as a part of his protective strength? She thought, with amusement, that Jamie would be just the man for her sister and would, undoubtedly, be wise to choose just such a woman. Not everyone would bear in silence his domineering manners, his lack of charm, his authoritarian outlook on life. It was ironic that he should wish to marry a spirited woman who was fearless, strong and capable. Such a marriage must result in a clash of wills.

The ball began a little late, some of the more important guests being unpunctual, but at last it opened with Charlotte and Tom dancing the first waltz together while the assembled guests, who were all aware of the reason for the ball, politely clapping them twice round the ballroom.

Sabrina's card was almost full when Johnny came up to request a dance. She had been hoping, despite herself, that he would come to her, and the shooting joy which filled her when she saw him approach was hard to disguise.

He took the card she held out, ran an eye down the names and frowned. "You are very much in demand," he said curtly, adding his own name at the end of the list.

He was very handsome in his evening clothes, his curly black hair well brushed, his broad shoulders accentuated by the cut of the tailcoat he wore.

She smiled at him politely, keeping her eyes slightly lowered to disguise the pleasure it gave her to look at him.

"There has been no news of Will Duckett?" she asked, hoping to keep him by her side a few moments longer.

He lingered, shaking his head. "No, nothing. I have been keeping my eyes open on my rounds, but I have seen no sign of him."

"Do you think he has . . ." she paused, not wishing to say aloud what was in her mind.

"Killed himself?" Johnny cut in. "No, I cannot believe it. He was too angry. A man like Will Duckett would not harm himself."

The emphasis of his words startled her. "You believe he may try to harm Mr. Link?"

"I would not be altogether surprised. The last time I saw him, Will was full of oaths of revenge. I thought he would calm down in the end. I am afraid I did not take him seriously enough. But after his attack on Link, I must revise my opinion."

"But Mr. Link was not much hurt, I thought," she said.

"He had two teeth broken and a very nasty black eye," Johnny said dryly. "He was very angry. It is just as well we did not find Will too soon—Link was baying for his blood. There would have been a charge laid against him."

"Have you seen Mrs. Duckett since she went into the Workhouse?" she asked, after a little pause.

"Once," he admitted. "They are not happy to have interference in their affairs, you know, so I have had to relinquish her as a patient. Their own medical officer is more than capable of delivering her child. But I did ride over to Theydon Garnon the day after she was taken in, and they let me see her briefly. She is very low, poor woman. Depressed, weak, very lethargic. They have not put her to any tasks in view of her condition, and she has little to do but brood upon her misfortunes."

"And her children?" asked Sabrina in pity.

"Taken from her, of course, and put into care. I did not see them. Rob, of course, is living in my house now. He seems to enjoy looking after my horse, and he certainly eats enough for ten boys. His separation from his mother does not seem to have affected him too much."

"It must weigh upon him," she protested, "a small boy of eight years, taken from his mother in such hard circumstances . . ."

Johnny looked at her intently, his eyes almost bewildered. "What a strange, unaccountable girl you are," he began, but was interrupted by Jamie, claiming her as his partner for the next dance.

Johnny stood back, bowing, and she was whirled away in Jamie's arms. Looking back, she saw Johnny watching them, his brows drawn together, but as their eyes met, he turned away.

"I have been watching you," Jamie said suddenly, and she was startled into a stumble.

"I am sorry, so sorry," she mumbled, then, "Watching me? How do you mean?"

"With the doctor," Jamie explained. "You were having such a very sober conversation. No smiles, none of the usual little gestures and pauses which one sees in polite society. I was curious to know the subject of such very intent exchanges."

She looked up and met the dryly curious gaze. "We were talking of a poor family of the neighborhood," she said, a little offhandedly. "They are in great trouble, and I have interested myself in them."

He looked approvingly at her. "That is what I am always glad to hear. Ladies should take an interest in the welfare of the poor. My own mother visits the crofts unsparingly."

"Indeed?" she said politely, wondering what reception her aunt would have were she to visit the villagers "unsparingly." She suspected the reception would not be jovial. The people of this district, so near the capital, so sophisticated compared with the more remote areas, must be more sensitive in their relationships with the other classes than were those of the far North.

She could only wonder, later, in talk with both Tom and Jamie, to see the lively, high-spirited Tom so obsequious to his stern cousin, to hear him defer to Jamie's decided opinions at every point. Human beings never failed to amaze her. Tom, who had rejected with wild defiance every attempt by his parents to influence or guide him, seemed eager to take over every one of Jamie's views as if they were handed down from heaven.

"You are quite right, Jamie," he cried, when his cousin made a scathing remark upon the flirtatious behavior of some young man nearby, "It is, indeed, ill bred to behave so." And he met Sabrina's wondering eye with a blithe smile, apparently completely unconscious of any reminder of his own late behavior.

She danced several times with Byrd, who was soothing company, in cheerful, good-humored spirits, sufficiently admiring of her dress to elevate her mood and content to talk or be silent as she pleased.

He made no mention of his proposal during the picnic at his farm, yet she felt his attention sometimes pressing upon her mind and caught him once or twice watching her with the expression of a proprietor, which made her frown, and draw away from him.

She had not allowed herself to seriously consider his proposal. On the surface, such an idea must be flattering. She was not likely to receive a better offer and must consider her future before it was too late. She could hardly wish to remain schoolmistress of Ambresbury all her life, a dowdy spinster of little means and no social life. Yet, even so, with all that self interest could advance, and all that her family and friends could most likely have to say upon the subject, she felt no real inclination to accept him.

I like him, she told herself, as they danced, and he is a kind, pleasant companion. But as a husband? It was mere romantc folly to wish for love in marriage. She was not so far gone in her idiocy to demand perfection. And yet . . .

When they halted beside Charity, sitting in a corner alone, playing cat's cradle with her fingers to appear occupied, Byrd looked at Sabrina, his eyebrows raised. "Has your sister no partners?" he asked very softly.

She shrugged. "I am afraid that may well be so," she whispered back.

"This cannot be allowed," he said, frowning, and advanced upon Charity, picking up her dance card with a quick smile.

She blushed to the hair, her eyes lifting in miserable anxiety to his face, then falling again.

"I see you have the next waltz free, Miss Charity," he said warmly. "Will you allow me the pleasure?"

Charity's small, pale face, as colorless in her white gown as if it had been in her black, suddenly quivered with some fierce emotion as she thanked him. Sabrina, watching casually, felt a quick premonition, and looked at her more closely. Had she misread that glance of her sister's? She had lately, she realized without comprehending it, been watching for some young man who would take over from her the responsibility of protecting Charity from the world's cold wind. Only today, she had decided Jamie might suit, but now, seeing her sister rise and tremblingly glide away in Byrd's arms, she accused herself of blindness.

Could she be mistaken now? That quick upward look, the hard flush on Charity's cheek just below the small cheekbones, the faint, wistful smile which came and went as Byrd spoke to her. Were all these only chance, or had Charity concealed from her for weeks a secret emotion?

She was so intent upon her thoughts that she jumped when Johnny spoke to her.

"Our dance, I believe?"

She turned, flushing, her heart suddenly beating so fast she felt certain he must hear it.

"Oh . . . yes . . ."

"You look flushed," he said, staring at her with hard eyes. "Are you hot?"

"No, no," she denied, terrified to consider the loss of this dance which had been so long looked forward to, the first they had ever had together.

He held out his arm, she laid her hand upon it, awkwardly aware that her fingers trembled visibly, and then she was held, his arm around her waist, her hand upon his shoulder, and they moved into the crowd.

She had never danced so badly. Every thought had fled from her mind except the all engrossing, all pervading, thought that she was once more, however formally, held in his arms.

He, too, appeared in no mood for idle talk. They danced in silence. She saw nothing of the other dancers. Her head, just reaching his shoulder, almost touched it. Her eyes were fixed in a blind, sensual stare, reflecting her intense physical delight. The excitement gave her a flush which emphasized the brightness of her eyes, and Johnny, glancing down, said suddenly, "You are not ill, are you?"

His voice broke her mood of abandonment to the pleasure of dancing with him. She looked up, blinking, her lips slightly parted, her expression dazed.

"I am sorry. What did you say?"

He was unreasonably angry. "I asked if you were ill," he said tensely. "You were so deep in thought you did not hear me, I suppose. Does it disturb you to see your sister and Johnstone dancing together so happily?"

She stared at him, in mounting rage, "I had not even noticed," she said, suddenly hating him for thinking such things of her.

"They look well together," he sneered.

She did not answer. Her happiness was shattered. Dragged back to reality, she stumbled as they danced, and he looked at her with disapproval.

He steered her towards the end of the ballroom where the door stood open into a glass-roofed conservatory into which some of the younger dancers occasionally disappeared for a moment or two. This practice was tolerated by their elders for so brief a time, but had to be carefully timed. Too long a stay was considered fast and was noticed.

Johnny released her and gestured forward. "Some cooler air will do you good."

She walked through into the long, domed room, among palms in tubs, and a heavy-scented array of geraniums, night stock and other flowers.

Another couple stood by the conservatory door, gazing out into the garden. The young man's arm was around the girl, and she was smiling. They turned, startled, as the newcomers walked by, and hurriedly retreated back to the ballroom.

Johnny watched them go with a cynical air. "Poor fool," he said, looking at her as if daring her to contradict.

She stood looking out at the dark blue sky, feeling strangely light-headed. The warm scents of the room, the shaded lights reflected from the ballroom off the windows, the soft swirl of the music which came to them all contributed to her mood.

He came and stood beside her, their shoulders touching. For a moment neither spoke. Then he said huskily, "You look very beautiful in white, Sabrina . . ."

His softened tone made her heart turn over. With caught breath, she looked up, eyes widened. "Thank you."

He put out a hand and softly touched the lace and ribbon which were caught at the top of her sleeve, lying over her bare shoulders in a tangle. His finger smoothed them out, then moved very slowly along her shoulder bone, to her throat.

Breath catching fiercely, she waited, passive under his touch, and when he turned her chin gently, looked up, with parted lips and eyes that did not rebuke.

He bent his head. This time he did not withdraw before their lips met, but took her lips hungrily, his arms sliding round her waist.

The moment of impact brought a rush of bitter passion. Her hands went up involuntarily to clutch at his curly black hair. She pressed closer, melting against him, releasing the pent-up urgency of months of frustration.

When at last he withdrew, she stood, chilled and depleted, emotionally drained, shivering as though she stood out in the dark, windy night.

He stared out of the window again, his profile stony. Then he turned and stared at her, shaking his head, as though puzzled.

"Johnny?" she asked, wondering what he was thinking.

"If I could understand you," he said tautly. "If I could believe in you . . ."

"Johnny," she began again, passionately, about to beg him to trust her, to believe what she told him, but at that moment Louisa came into the conservatory, scowling and flouncing, and stared at them both with jealous eyes.

"Sabrina, Mama is looking for you," she said.

Sabrina drew away from Johnny and said, "Where is she?"

"In the chaperone's corner," Louisa told her in a voice sullen with suspicion, resentment and distrust.

Sabrina curtsied to Johnny and hurried away. The lights of the ballroom struck upon her eyes, dazzling her. The music seemed too loud, the colors too bright, the people too frivolous.

Aunt Maria surveyed her with frozen displeasure. "Where have you been, Miss?" she hissed, holding her fan so that nobody else should hear. "You went into the conservatory with Dr. Graham at least fifteen minutes ago. Are you determined to ruin his reputation and your own?"

Sabrina murmured something, she did not know herself what, feeling as if she had been far, far away, caught up in some experience too intense to comprehend, and while still deeply involved, had been wrenched back to a cold, dull world.

Aunt Maria's face was bitter. "You have been nothing but trouble since you came to us," she said, "the most disruptive influence we could have brought into our circle. I am glad that you will soon leave Ambreys forever."

"I am sorry you feel like that," Sabrina managed.

Her aunt gave her a look of dislike bordering on real hatred. "You need not think Dr. Graham will look in your direction," she said. "He may have flirted with you. Men often do with girls like you, but he would never marry you. You have neither fortune nor friends. And Dr. Graham is far too sensible to marry to disoblige his family. He is too conscious of his position."

"I am sure you are right," said Sabrina fiercely, touched on a tender spot, and then she turned and walked away.

Byrd caught her arm as she moved through the press of people. "Sabrina, what is it? You look ill."

Charity was with him, still flushed and with shining eyes. The look of almost radiance died out as she saw her sister, and Sabrina thought bitterly that even with Charity she was more of an obstacle than a friend. Her earlier conjecturing was clearly accurate. Charity's feelings for Byrd were warm, and from her face, she saw Sabrina as a rival.

With an effort which cost her dearly, Sabrina pretended cheerfulness and remained in their company for the rest of the evening.

The betrothal announcement was made, toasts drunk, a great deal of laughter and teasing inflicted upon the happy pair. The dancing recommenced. Sabrina danced once more with Jamie, listened politely to his pronouncements, was whirled away by Byrd when Jamie released her, and danced with him like a wooden doll.

"You are very quiet tonight," he said, looking down at her face.

"Am I?" she tried to smile. "It is late," she added, "perhaps I am tired. I was up early this morning."

Softly, he asked, "Have you thought about what I said to you down by the river, Sabrina? When will I have an answer?"

Chilled and unhappy, she was less gentle than she might have been. "I am sorry, Byrd," she said, in dull tones, "I am very sorry."

His arm tightened. "Do I take it that you are refusing me?" he asked, in a voice which held surprise.

She nodded. "I am very grateful to you for asking me," she added, "but I cannot accept."

He was silent. Looking up, she saw his expression

clearly. There was no grief there, no pain or misery, only a look of wounded pride, perhaps, of regret, a frown of incomprehension. It was obvious that Byrd found her refusal puzzling. He had offered believing she would accept, feeling the honor he did her in asking her. He was insulted that she refused. A girl of her background, without money, would look far for another marriage to compare with the one he had offered.

All this she read in his face. "You do not love me, Byrd," she said, involuntarily, half apologizing.

He looked down at her, his brows rising. "Did I lead you to believe I did? I admire you; I respect you. A marriage founded on such a basis must be successful."

"Wait for love, Byrd," she murmured gently. "I am sure you will find it if you look about you." She could give him no clearer hint without betraying her sister.

He looked bewildered, a little affronted.

"And you?" he asked sharply, "is love what you are waiting for? I had thought more of you. Love is for fairy tales. From my own experience, love causes more unhappiness in marriage than any other single cause. Love matches are often disastrous."

"Perhaps," she conceded, "but without love, marriage is a mockery. I will wait and take my chance of losing everything. It is a gamble, but then I am a gambler."

For some reason this amused him. He threw back his head and laughed, drawing the attention of the nearest dancers upon them. Lowering his voice, he whispered, "A gambler, are you, Sabrina? Well, I will wish you luck, but I think you a foolish roman-tic, after all, and I have no great faith in your fate."

Over his shoulder, her eyes met those of Johnny, the dark blue stare cold and reserved. Her spirits sank again. "Neither have I, Byrd," she said sadly, "neither have I."

CHAPTER NINE

After such an exciting and exhausting period spent away from home in the company of mere acquaintances, it was natural that all the members of the Wilton family should be both glad and relieved to be back home, the party behind them, with its attendant joys and miseries.

A certain irritable tendency filled most of them. They were inclined to snap on the smallest provocation. Each seemed eager to be alone, returning to his or her normal pursuits without the wish for company which was normal in them all. Uncle Matthew, of course, had always preferred to be left to himself, rarely spending a morning or afternoon in the house. But even his wife now retired to her own room and asked only to be left alone.

Sabrina was doubly glad, now, of her little cottage in the village. She drove down in the trap on the morning after their return from Colling Grange and found Molly waiting for her with the kettle singing over the fire and a plate of home made scones upon the table.

"Have you heard anything of your father, Molly?" she asked, as she sat down with a sigh of pleasure before the table.

Molly waited upon her, pouring the tea and buttering the scones deftly. "No, Miss. Rob has been watching for Da, but there has been no sign. We reckon as how he's gone to London." Her tone was admiring, wistful. "That's where I'd go if I had the chance."

Sabrina smiled at her. "Would you, Molly? Why?"

The child's eyes shone. "Shops and people, Miss. Once we walked over to High Beech, and from a little hill we saw the spires of London churches. Leastwise, Da said they were. Stretches for miles, London does, seemingly."

"Yes," said Sabrina, "it is a big city. But you are better off here, at Ambresbury, Molly. London is a dirty place. The streets are very narrow, and the houses are too close together. You would be unhappy there."

"Not me, Miss," said Molly defiantly. "I'd get a fine place in a great house, and wear a uniform, and have followers."

Sabrina laughed. "Would you, indeed?" She wondered what her aunt would say if she could hear this conversation. Aunt Maria would be shocked and baffled. The servants at Ambreys were like children, seen but not heard, moving about the house on soft, discreet feet, performing their duties without ever impinging upon the consciousness of their mistress. Aunt Maria would no more have discussed London with her new scullery maid than she would have jumped off the top of the house.

"Your sister, Nan, is settling in well at Ambreys," she told Molly. "She has a half day once a fortnight, on a Wednesday. I have spoken to her and told her she may come down here for tea on those days. She has nowhere else to go, poor child, now that your home is broken up."

Molly thanked her. "D'you think we'll ever be together again, Miss?" she asked anxiously. "They will let my Mam out one day, won't they?"

Sabrina assured her that they would, without much conviction herself. If Will Duckett remained missing, there would be no husband to set up a home for the family when the employment situation improved.

To Johnny, whom she saw that afternoon, she said that Molly's attitude toward the Workhouse was one of fear and distrust. "She speaks of it as if it had a personality, was a thinking object. Rather as she might speak of a wolf lurking in the woods."

"It has much the same character," he agreed. "It haunts the back of their minds. Once stumble, and it has got you."

They were making arrangements for the physical welfare of the children who were to attend the school. Johnny was to inspect them for lice in their hair and give them a lecture on personal hygiene. "Half of them never wash," he said cheerfully, "but you must be firm upon that point. They must wash, even if only in cold water, every day. And their clothes must be clean. It is not only to learn to read and write that they are coming here."

"It must be very hard to wash when every bucket of water has to be brought by hand from the pump," she said thoughtfully. "I suppose it would not be possible to make arrangements for them to wash at school?"

"There is no room," he pointed out, "and I imagine the board would complain that they were wasting valuable time."

She sighed. "Their lives are very hard."

"Harder than you suspect," he said. "You should come with me on my rounds and see them in their homes. Childbirth and death are everyday sights to these children. The crowded conditions in which they live make them so. Your Aunt Maria would be utterly horrified if Louisa caught a small glimpse of the sort of things these children see."

She smiled. "I am sure you are right."

He was called out a moment later to visit the sick wife of a cottager in a remote part of the forest. Sabrina stood at the window and watched him ride off on his mare, the boy who had come for him up behind, waving gleefully to the village women in their usual place at the pump.

She was so engrossed in what she was doing that the afternoon wore on, unnoticed, and it was only when Molly came in to light the lamp that she realized that it was almost dusk.

"I must go," she said, in alarm, "I shall be late for dinner if I do not hurry."

Molly brought her bonnet and cloak, and Sabrina left for Ambreys, setting the pony at a fast trot, hoping that her long absence would not further irritate Aunt Maria.

The dinner hour was sacred at Ambreys. Punctuality was regarded as a great virtue, and Uncle Matthew would be scathing if she were late.

She was on the long road uphill, past the stone bridge, when a small figure dropped down out of a field, scrambling through the hawthorn with a tearing of cloth, and hailed her.

She drew in the pony, recognizing Rob, and smiled at him. His face was grimy, his shirt and trousers muddy and torn.

"Have you been playing in the forest, Rob?" she asked with indulgence.

She knew that Johnny allowed the boy great freedom. He had told her that afternoon that Rob was off somewhere by himself and said, "He is too young to be caged all day. Boys need to roam about from time to time. He is always there when I need him, and what he does when he has finished his work in the stable is no business of mine. A boy of eight cannot be treated as a grown man."

Rob was panting, his thin chest heaving with his exertions. He tried to speak, but the words were inaudible.

"Wait a moment, wait a moment," she laughed. "You are out of breath. Wait until you can speak before you try again."

He drew a ragged breath. "Miss, I seen my Da!" he cried.

She stiffened and stared at him. "Where, Rob?"

"In the forest. Up Epping Thicks way, near the Banks."

She understood his description. This was very near where she and Johnny had paused that day in the storm. The forest there was deep, tangled and lonely. Very few people ever went into it, and only the foresters knew its paths.

"Did you speak to him?"

Rob nodded. "Aye, I did. I called to him."

"And what did he say to you?" she asked, anxious, yet trying to sound calm for the sake of the child.

"Asked me how I was, whether the Doctor was treating me right." Rob grinned at her. "I told him the Doctor was treating me like a king. Three meals a day and new clothes, and he lets me groom his mare every day."

"And then what did your father say, Rob?"

"He said as that was good. He told me to behave myself and do just what the Doctor said, and as I should be grateful to him for being so kind." He looked indignant for a moment, "And I am, Miss. I always behave myself. Doctor only once shouted at me, I told Da, and that was when I climbed on the stable roof after the cat, and he thought I'd fall down. Right roaring mad, Doctor was. You should 'ave seen his eyes flash, Miss."

Sabrina smiled, thinking how Johnny's eyes looked when they were angry. Then, more seriously, she asked, "But what is your father doing, Rob, in the forest? Surely he has not been there all this time?"

Rob's face grew pale; his eyes were anxious as he looked up at her. "He said as how I wasn't to tell, Miss. He said he'd skin me alive if I so much as breathed a word to a soul. But I'm worried . . . I don't think it's right . . ."

She gave him her hand and helped him up into the trap. "Tell me, Rob," she ordered.

He looked over his shoulder quickly, as though fearing listening ears, "You won't split?"

"If I think I ought to, Rob, I must tell someone— Doctor Graham, perhaps. You would trust Doctor Graham, wouldn't you?"

Rob thought about it. "Yes," he said doubtfully, "I think I would. And it isn't right, what my Da means to do . . . He frightened me . . ."

"Your father is not himself at the moment, Rob," she said sadly. "Worry has made him ill. I think you should tell me."

He lowered his voice and put his mouth close to her ear. "He means to set fire to Sweet Briars, Miss. Tonight. The haymaking is finished, and the ricks are stacked. My Da is going to set light to them, and to the house, and burn it to the ground. He said he doesn't care if he goes up with it so long as Farmer Link goes, too."

She went pale. "Oh, no, he must not! It is madness!"

Rob looked up at her, shivering, his small face drawn and white. "Miss, do you think my Da really is mad? He looked very strange in the forest."

She put an arm around him and hugged him, stroking back the hair from his face. "He is not himself, Rob. He needs help."

"What will you do?" Rob asked.

"We must get Dr. Graham to him," she said. "He will know what to do." And then she remembered that Johnny was out on a visit. She did not even know to which cottage he had been called. It was, she remembered, somewhere remote and isolated. It would take time to get a message to him, even if she could find out whose cottage he was visiting.

She looked at Rob. "When will your father go to Sweet Briars, Rob? Did he say?"

"Tonight, after dark," he said.

She looked up at the sky. The sun had already set,

and the air was dusky. The trees were mere sketched outlines on the horizon; the birds had ceased to call. A lone rook flapped across the field beside them and settled, cawing, in the top of a swaying elm.

"It will soon be dark," she said anxiously. How would Johnny find Will Duckett in the dark forest?

Rob quivered in the circle of her arms. "And there are those others . . ." he muttered.

She looked sharply at him, "Others? Which others?"

"I don't know," he said, whispering. "I saw them, through the trees, sitting round a fire. My Da walked me away from them. I don't know who they were."

"Woodmen, perhaps," she said thoughtfully. "Someone must have been feeding and sheltering him. There is probably more than one charcoal burner's hut in the forest which would give him shelter."

She looked up at the sky again and made a decision. "Rob," she said, "I think I might persuade your father not to do this. Will you show me where he was?"

Rob wriggled in her arms. "Oh, Miss, I dursen't. He will be livid."

"You want him helped, though, Rob?" she said.

"Yes, Miss, but I couldn't, I couldn't come . . ."

She sighed. "Then tell me exactly where he was, and I will go alone. You must run back to the village and find Doctor Graham. Get a message to him, somehow, and tell him what you have told me now. Tell him I have gone to talk to your father, to persuade him out of this plan of revenge."

"I will, Miss," he agreed, and gave her a careful

guide to the spot where he had last seen his father.

She put him down on the road and smiled at him. "Run as fast as you can, Rob," she said, "and do not tell anyone but Doctor Graham what you have told me." She knew what short shrift Will Duckett would get from the villagers if they thought he was lurking in the woods with mad ideas of vengeance in his brain.

"Miss," Rob called uneasily, "be careful, Miss. Da's got his shotgun with him."

She shivered. "I know," she said bravely, smiling back at him, but her nerves jumped violently at the recollection. How sane was Will Duckett after several weeks in the forest, brooding on his wrongs, half starving, probably, wet, cold, miserable? She could not believe that he would shoot her or harm her in any way, but she had one tiny corner of doubt in her mind which haunted her as she drove past the gate of Ambreys and up the hill which led to Epping Thicks.

As the sky continued to darken, the forest took on a somber aspect, looming above her, shadowy, strange, alien. There were no houses on this narrow lane, and the trap was only just able to pass along, scraping the banks on either side. It was little but a cart track, rutted, uneven and hedged on either side. On one side lay the forest, on the other a field under pasture, full of grazing cows who ambled about slowly, still feeding even at this late hour.

She started violently when one put its head over the hedge and mooed at her. She recovered instantly, but that small shock had undermined her courage, and when she drew her trap into the side of the lane she sat for a moment, summoning her reserves of spirit, before she climbed down and carefully tethered the pony to a branch.

Epping Thicks had not acquired its name lightly. In this part of the forest, the holly grew thickly, choking the paths and making them narrow, twisting and in places impassable.

The weather had been very warm and dry for weeks. The grass was tall, bleached and feathery under her hands as she pushed her way up the bank into the forest.

A moth fluttered up from the grass, the circles on its wings like black eyes staring at her through the dusk.

Her heart was beating fast; her palms were both damp and cold. When something rustled in the holly thickets, she stopped dead in her tracks, holding her breath. Then a mouse ran across the path, halted at sight of her, and was gone in a flash, as frightened as herself. She smiled involuntarily and went on, elbowing her way between the clutching leaves, glad of her full skirts to protect her against the armored holly.

She had never been out alone at night before. In other circumstances, she might have been fascinated by what she saw and heard, but she was too frightened of what might lie ahead to be able to relax and look around her. All she wanted was to find Will Duckett and get out of the forest. The consequences of what he proposed alarmed and horrified her. At the very least there must be serious loss of property, at the worst a loss of life. And for Will Duckett, if he were caught, the sentence would be heavy. He would most probably hang.

She climbed up the overgrown banks, pausing every now and then to listen. In here, under the trees, the light had almost gone. There was no moon yet to show her the path, and she stumbled and fell once or twice, sliding down, bruising herself on a protruding root and catching the hem of her gown.

Rob had given her the general direction in which to walk, but in the darkness she might so easily lose her way. She was afraid to call out for fear of alarming Will Duckett and making him do something foolish. She would not allow herself to dwell on the subject of his shotgun, but it was present in her mind as she pushed her way along.

The ground had risen steeply here. She had to go on hands and knees, her nails scraping at the sides of the banks. With the night mist, the scent of the earth rose, damp and rich. She paused, panting, in the lee of a great beech tree, and waited to get back her breath. The melancholy moan of an owl some yards away made her jump and cling to the beech, shuddering. It came again, long drawn out, philosophical, floating down through the invisible whispering leaves. She wondered if she was too late. Would Will Duckett still be hiding here, or would he already be on his way to Sweet Briars?

Her doubts were answered a moment later, as she half slid, half ran down a steep incline into one of the long, curving moats between the Banks. These were full of decayed leaves, rotting slowly, making the moats soft underfoot. She felt her foot sink a little and cried out, cutting her cry short.

There was a sound from above her on the next bank, and then two figures leaped down, so suddenly that she had only a confused, terrified impression of dark bulk falling upon her, and then she was knocked to the ground, stifled under a heavy weight. She struggled, screaming soundlessly against a jacketed arm.

"Hey, Jack, 'tis a woman," said a deep voice, and she shuddered under a quick, exploratory hand, running over her breasts and then being removed.

She was pulled to her feet, a lantern shone into her face.

"Who're you, then? What're you doing here at this hour?" asked the man holding the lantern.

"I . . . I am looking for Will Duckett . . ." she said, guessing these to be the men whom Rob had seen with his father.

They looked at each other, their heads held well away from the yellow gleam of the lantern, so that all she could see was two ragged shapes.

"You're not his wife," said one.

"What d'ye want with 'un?" asked the other.

"Just a word," she whispered quickly. "I am here to help him. Please, if you know where he is, take me to him. He knows me."

They withdrew a little, to confer, and came back in a moment. "Follow me," said the one with the lantern, and took her arm.

The other sprang up the bank before them and vanished into the enveloping darkness. For a few seconds she heard his feet moving over leaves and twigs, a faint crackling sound, and then silence.

She was aided up the bank and then gestured to follow the wide curve to the right.

Ambresbury Banks ran in a succession of these

curves, like a pool after a stone has been thrown in,
the waves of earth radiating out from some unknown
center, broken at intervals by gaps, with the deep
moats between each earthen bank. They had had
some defensive purpose once, and now, she guessed,
they were used again for the same reason.

Soon, through the trees, she caught the red, misty
flicker of a fire, and started, remembering Johnny's
story of the local legends of the ghost fires of the
Iceni. Then she realized that this was no spiritual
manifestation, but a real fire, the one described to
her by Rob. She was nearing the camp of these men.

When she came into the firelight, she found a
number of shadowy forms standing back against the
trees, out of the red glare. She paused, gazing round,
her heart thumping.

Danger made her hair freeze on her head. She was
suddenly aware that she was alone here, at night,
with a number of strangers, mysterious dwellers in
the forest who guarded their camp and were jealous
of their secrets.

She spoke, not realizing how her voice trembled,
until she heard it, rusty and creaking, "Will? Will
Duckett?"

A disembodied voice which seemed vaguely familiar spoke from behind a tree, "Who is it? Stand
out where I can see you . . ."

The man with the lantern held it up to illumine
her face. A sigh came from the circle of men as her
white features and gleaming hair came into view.
She was conscious of a quick stir and forward move
among them.

Shaking, she called, "Will, you know me . . ."

He came out then and stood, facing her. She stared, her eyes huge. He looked strange, terrifying, like a creature from another world. He had blacked his face and wore a woollen cap on his head, pulled down to his eyes. His clothes were dark, muddy, disheveled.

"What do you want here, Miss?" he growled. "Rob told you, did he? I'll skin him when I see him."

"Will, I must speak with you," she said, urgency in her tone, "Please . . ."

"I'm listening," he said gruffly.

"Not here," she said, looking round at the black blurs of faces which watched her, their eyes gleaming white in their black faces. They were all dressed like Will, their skin blackened, their heads covered by similar woollen caps.

"My brothers can hear what you have to say," he said.

"Brothers?" she echoed, uncomprehending.

"We're all in it," he said, "they and I, all farm laborers who've been turned off and have only the workhouse to look to . . ."

She looked again around the circle, shivering convulsively. Now she felt her danger more keenly. She had risked her life in coming here. These were fierce, wolfish creatures, in the dark forest, plotting bloody deeds. She had come here to persuade a sick, bewildered man to abandon his plan of revenge, and she found the case far otherwise.

Will was not mad. He was abandoned to hatred.

She drew a deep breath and squared her shoulders. She could not go back, so she might as well do what she had come here to do. Otherwise it was all wasted effort.

"Will, you cannot burn down the farm," she said rapidly. "If you were caught you would be hanged . . ."

"I don't care for that!" he retorted. "Let them hang me. They cannot harm me more than they have done already."

"They have not murdered you," she protested, "but you may murder Mr. Link, or his wife, or little Emily, if you set fire to their farm."

"I don't intend for to leave them inside," he said. "We shall order them out when we have fired the place."

"Mr. Link will fight," she said.

He bent and held up a long thin object. "Not with my gun on his back," he said simply.

"Oh, Will," she said, "think of your wife, your children . . ."

"Did he think of them before he turned me off?"

"But to destroy everything on the farm," she cried.

"He took my livelihood away. I shall take his."

"And the other men? Your old friends who will be in the same case as yourself if you destroy the farm? You will put another six men into the work-house, Will, and their families."

"I can't help that," he said stubbornly; "we must teach the farmers a lesson. We must stand together and suffer together. A man should not be forced into the workhouse for no crime but being no longer wanted."

"Mr. Link could not afford to keep you," she said.

"He could afford to keep a fat pony for his daughter and buy his wife silk dresses," said Will angrily.

"I've had enough of this," said one of the others, moving into the firelight. He was a big man, his head like that of a bull, lowered and menacing, his eyes shining white and round as he approached them. "She's said her piece, Will. Now she must pay for her nosy interference . . ."

As he spoke, he grabbed Sabrina, who cried out in terror as his huge hand clamped down on her mouth. Holding her, wriggling and kicking, he called for the others to help him.

In a moment, she was tied by the wrists and the feet and dumped unceremoniously on the ground by a tree, her mouth gagged with a handkerchief which smelled of onions and made her eyes water.

"What are you going to do with her?" Will asked with what she hoped was anxiety.

They were silent for a moment. Then one said, "Who is she, Will? Some farmer's daughter? How did she come to know you were here, then?"

"She's the village schoolmistress," Will told them. "My eldest, Molly, is her maid. She's been good to my children, I'll say that. I'd want no harm to come to her. She means well enough."

"Has she come alone?" he was asked.

"Joe went back to check. He says there's nothing stirring back to the road. There's a pony and trap tied up on by Epping Thicks track. Hers, he reckons."

"Well? What shall we do with her?"

"We won't be coming back here," said the bull-headed man slowly. "I say we leave her here, tied as she is, and let her be found in the morning. Too late by then for anyone to stop us."

"Suppose she told someone she was coming here," protested another man. "We've got to have time to get safely away from Sweet Briars."

"What? Who would let a woman come here at this hour?" sneered the bullheaded man. "No, she's come alone, and no one knows but Rob Duckett." He turned to Will, "What of Rob? Will he have told the whole village, Will?"

Will shook his head. "I guess he told my Molly and she told her mistress," he said. "That would be the way of it."

"We've wasted too much time on her," growled another man. "I vote we go now and get it over with. I want to be away from here as soon as I can."

"Aye," they agreed, "let's go now. Even if she told nobody she was coming, someone may see her pony and trap and come looking . . ."

"We could let it free," suggested the bullheaded man, "that would delay the searchers."

This was agreed. "It will find its way back to the stables," they said.

Another moment and the fire was kicked out, the lantern withdrew among the trees, most of the men with it, and Will bent over her.

"I'm sorry, Miss, but we've no choice but to leave you here. You would have done better to mind your own business. You'll be found, don't fret. Rob and Molly will come for you before the morning, I'm sure."

She made frantic noises, terrified of being left

here in the dark, bound as she was, and unable to scream out when help did arrive.

But Will shuffled off after his fellows, and in a moment the sound of their movements was gone, and the silence of the forest settled in upon her.

CHAPTER TEN

In the silence she began to hear each separate little sound with acute attention. The creak of the branches in the wind, the rustle of the leaves, and the whispering grasses bending as the wind passed over them, soon became distinguishable. The owls which haunted the forest were calling now, in the belief that the humans who had invaded their night territory had all gone, and she looked up at the trees, hearing their sad, strange notes distinctly, shivering through the leaves, and fancied for a moment that she saw a blundering among the lower branches of an oak, the flash of a silver eye as the great wings folded.

Around her she heard the scamper of the owl's prey, some tiny rodent finding sanctuary in a tree root, or under a bush.

She was uncomfortable, contorted by the posture which her bonds forced her to assume, her hands tied behind her back, her feet tied together, leaning back against the tree, staring with widened, alert eyes at the darkness.

She had never realized before how dark it was in the forest at night. But as the time went by, and her eyes grew accustomed to it, she began to pick out variations of shadow. A bush looked like a deer, horned head stooped; another seemed to twist towards her like a snake, and on a third a pinpoint of moonlight glittered now and then, giving her some contact with the outside world.

To comfort herself, she listened for the sound of Johnny coming to free her. Surely he must come soon. Rob must have found him by now. He would climb onto his mare and gallop here to rescue her, like young Lochinvar, and carry her off on the back of his steed, his arms around her. She closed her eyes, weak at the thought, and warmth filled her.

Her happiness at this image kept her cheerful for some while, but gradually the chill air of the night crept back; she shivered, stared about her, trying to penetrate the distant shapes of the bushes and trees.

What was Johnny doing?

Suppose Rob had not found him or had forgotten to look? How long would she be here? She was already stiff and cold. By morning she would, she began to think, have suffocated too, for the onion smell of the handkerchief gagging her was oppressive and choking.

Her heart began to pound unpleasantly. A cold perspiration broke out on her temples and trickled down her face. She longed to wipe it away but was helpless.

She moved her hands, which were becoming numb, and felt a shooting pain through her wrists. Her feet, too, were tingling uncomfortably, and she shuffled them about to try to help her circulation.

She wondered if she might dare to try to stand up. She made a few exploratory movements, then desisted. The bank here was so steep that she was afraid she might fall down into the moat and injure herself if she tried to stand up. /

Her thoughts moved to Sweet Briars. Would the rioters have reached it yet? She imagined the horror of the family when the black-visaged men burst in upon them, finding them perhaps in bed asleep, and ordered them out. What would Farmer Link do? Would he stand, as they ordered, and watch, while they burned his home and his ricks? Or would he attempt to fight them? And if he did, would Will Duckett shoot him as he had threatened?

She shivered, thinking of his child, Emily. She was pert, spoiled, selfish, but she was only eight years old, and such an experience must mark her for life.

Will Duckett's children would not easily forget the shame and misery of life in the workhouse, but two wrongs did not make a right. Violent cures were often worse than the disease, as Papa had always said when he talked of the French Revolution.

She remembered listening to Uncle Matthew only a short time ago, furiously denouncing some farm laborers in the far eastern part of Essex who had rioted and burned hayricks while their fellow workers watched with tears in their eyes as their own homes and livelihoods went up in smoke.

She sighed. There seemed no answer to it. Life was a hard, cruel business for these people, whichever way they turned. To Uncle Matthew, the Golden Age was the Napoleonic War, when English farmers grew fat and rich, and there was always work for a man who needed it.

She wondered how long she had been here. Her numb, frozen hands and feet seemed to say that she had been here for many hours. It was impossible to guess. She only knew that she was cold, unhappy, frightened.

She sat up, pressing back against a tree, as she heard a slow rustle, then the crack of a twig.

Johnny, she thought in hope.

But surely he would call out for her, he would not creep along making so little noise. She listened intently, every nerve tingling. Was that the scrape of a heel on the stony earth at her back? If only her feet were not tied, if only she were not gagged!

A figure loomed up beside the tree. She stared up through the misty darkness, then began kicking and making muffled cries of joy, pleading, warning.

Johnny knelt, exclaiming, and in a moment had removed her gag.

"Johnny," she sobbed, and felt salt in her mouth as the tears she had not noticed ran into her parted lips.

His arms went round her, held her, pressing her head into his shoulder.

"You came," she muttered damply on his coat. "You were so long!"

He held her a little away, began to rub her hands, saw the bonds, and quickly untied them. "Good God," he said furiously, "did Will Duckett do this to you?"

"And my feet," she said incoherently.

He loosed them, and took each into his hands, rubbing them until she begged him to stop.

"They hurt," she explained, moving them about gently until the agony of the returning blood eased a little. Then he helped her to stand, and she leaned against him, stifling a groan of pain.

"Are you hurt?" he asked, catching her by the shoulders.

"Only where they tied me," she explained.

"They? There were others? My God, Sabrina, you must have been mad to come here like this. What did they do to you?"

"Nothing, except tie me up," she soothed. "I had to come. Will is going to set fire to Sweet Briars tonight. I tried to stop him." She sighed. "I was no use, though. I could not think of the word to say that might stop him. He was set on his revenge."

"Who were these others?" he demanded.

"Farm workers like Will. Turned off from their places. They had blackened their faces to avoid being recognized. I did not know any of them."

He seemed stunned. "My God," he said again, fiercely, "to think of you, here, alone, in this place, with men like that . . ."

"Yes, but Johnny, we must get help. Sweet Briars will burn to the ground. What shall we do?"

"You think they really mean to do it?" he asked. "I cannot believe Will would do such a wicked thing."

"He is so angry," she said helplessly. "I am sure they meant to do it, Johnny, and they went a very long time ago."

"I sent Rob to Ambreys," he said. "I dropped him off on my way here. He was to tell your uncle and have help sent to Sweet Briars, just in case."

"Do you think he will do it, though? He would not wish to betray his father."

Johnny shrugged. "There is no time to worry over that. We must get to Sweet Briars ourselves. Whatever has happened, there will be work to do. Where is your pony and trap? I did not see it on the road. How did you get here?"

She explained that the men had let the pony go free to delay any rescuers.

"Then I shall have to take you up on my mare," he said. "Can you bear to come with me? I cannot leave you here, and if I take you to Ambreys I will lose valuable time."

"I shall be better with you," she said. "I was so frightened here, alone. I did not know what a coward I was until tonight. Every little sound terrified me."

He made a choked sound, she thought of laughter, and bent. Before she knew what he was doing, he had swept her up into his arms and was carrying her away, down the banks and up again, walking warily, her weight balanced against his chest.

She lay very still, warmed by his closeness, her heart thudding as she felt his arms tighten. It seemed a very little while before they emerged from Epping Thicks into the lane. His mare stood there, tethered and grazing quietly.

Johnny lifted her up on to the mare's back, side saddle, and then sprang up behind her, gathered up the reins and urged the mare forward. Her double burden seemed to give her no difficulty. She trotted away willingly enough and began to pick up speed as they descended the hill.

Sabrina glanced up at the sky. The moon was up now, floating slowly through pale wreaths of cloud. The sight was peculiarly pleasant after her long enclosure in the dark forest, giving her a feeling of security and ease. She could not avoid the comparison. She had been immured in darkness and was now relieved to be once more out in the light.

The wind was gentle on her face, ruffling her hair; the air came sweet and fresh to her lungs. She breathed deeply.

Johnny glanced down, and his arm tightened until he held her firmly, his knee resting along hers, her body held in the crook of his arm. "You are looking more like yourself," he said quietly.

She felt tears prick her eyes at the kindness of his tone. She longed to express the emotions which were rising in her. Yielding to the covering indifference of the night, she turned her face into his shoulder like a child, confident in this moment of not being repulsed, and his only response was to tighten his hold on her yet more. They rode on in this calm mood until they were a mile from Sweet Briars.

She felt Johnny's muscles tense in the arm which held her, and she sat up, staring at the sky. A red glare was growing, like the last gleams of an autumn sun, above the farm buildings they were approaching.

"They have done it," Johnny said starkly.

She could not answer. A convulsive shudder ran through her as she wondered what they would find when they arrived.

Johnny kicked at the mare, shouting to her, and she put on a fresh spurt of speed. Galloping along the grassy track which ran to the farm, they took the closed gate without a halt, although the mare lurched and skidded on the muddy path which ran along the side of the house. As they rounded the corner, the scene leapt out at them, an etching in black and red, illumined by the leaping flames.

The Link family stood facing them, huddled together in the yard, the child clutched in her mother's arms, her face a white blur, a shawl roughly pulled over her long nightgown. Somehow the sight of her small, naked feet beneath the white folds of her gown made Sabrina's eyes fill with tears once more. There was a pathetic vulnerability about the child, her pertness gone, submerged by fear and bewilderment.

Her mother was sobbing, bent forward as if to protect the child, her long hair loose and tangled.

Mr. Link stood beside them, staring at his burning house, his arms folded. Rage, bitterness, hatred, gave him a manic look of barely controlled savagery. The very muscles of his shoulders seemed reined in by the merest thread. He seemed taller, broader, almost elemental in his fury, as if about to burst into violent action at any moment. Sabrina saw that his wife kept one hand upon his arm all the time, as if restraining him.

As the mare came round the corner, Sabrina took all this in with a comprehensive glance, but the frozen tableau lasted only a moment. The little group stared at her and Johnny as they stared back in shocked surprise.

Then the mare made a shrill snorting sound of terror, jerking backwards in alarm at the sight of the flames, and another movement snatched at Sabrina's attention.

She suddenly saw Will Duckett standing a little apart from the Link family, a shotgun trained on them. He had started violently as the newcomers arrived, and the barrel jerked upwards.

"Stay where you are, Doctor," he said, moving so that he could bring them under his eyes. "I will shoot the child if anyone moves, I warn you! If you value her life, stay where you are!"

Mrs. Link cried, "Oh, help us . . . my God, help us!"

Johnny sat the mare like a rock, staring at Will. "Are you out of your mind, Will? Do you know what the penalty for arson is? You will be hanged, or transported."

"That's my business," Will growled, "you shouldn't have come here, Doctor. Keep out of this. I've nothing against you, but I'll brook no interference."

"What you are doing is wrong, Will," Johnny said calmly. "You know it! You achieve nothing by this but to make things worse for yourself and your family. How will they ever get out of the workhouse if you are hanged? This is a terrible crime you are committing. Worse than what has been done to you. You are taking away the homes and livelihoods of your old friends, not just revenging yourself on Mr. Link."

"Now you see that I was right," Mr. Link said furiously. "He is a dangerous scoundrel, just as I always said. You befriended him, Doctor! Now see what you have done! Encouraged him to think himself wrongly treated, encouraged him to believe he had a right to revenge. And now, when it is too late, you realize how wrong you were!"

"I have never encouraged him to think of revenge," Johnny said angrily. "No Christian could."

"Shut your noise," Will growled. "It is done now. I take nothing back."

Mr. Link's teeth snapped tight together, giving him a look of wolf-like ferocity, his lips drawn back in a snarl. But his wife's imploring hand held back whatever action he contemplated, and he fell silent.

They all stared at Will, who glared back, his shot-gun held unwaveringly on the child.

The house was burning fiercely now. The wind fanned the flames, which were most apparent on the ground floor, but were spreading upwards rapidly. The glass in the lower windows was cracked and had showered out on to the neat flowerbeds beneath. Flames shot out through them, tonguing the air.

A timber suddenly cracked, showering sparks with a little spitting explosion of sound which brought Will's head swinging involuntarily to look.

Johnny took the opportunity. Sabrina's heart thudded painfully as he slid down from the mare's back, keeping its body between himself and Will, and silently moved into the shadows behind them. She kept very still, hoping Will would not hear him, but she saw that Will was too absorbed in watching the fire to notice.

She wondered where the other fire-raisers had gone. Had they lost courage before reaching Sweet Briars, or had they left as soon as the fire had been started, frightened of being caught?

She remembered the tense nervousness with which they had behaved in the forest, and suspected the latter. Any man caught on such a criminal venture would suffer the extreme penalty under the law. Fire-raising was a very serious crime.

She glanced at the Link family and saw Mr. Link watching Will closely. The intentness with which he waited, his head leaning forward, like a bull pushing at a gate, his body poised on the balls of his feet, made her realize that he had noticed Johnny creep away and was alert for some signal for action.

Just then Johnny appeared in the shadows on the far side of Will. She saw him gesture with his hand to Farmer Link, and saw the other man nod.

Mrs. Link had seen Johnny too, and her pale face seemed to grow paler than ever. She convulsively clutched her child to her, trembling, her eyes fixed in terror on Will's gun.

Sabrina's skin was icy cold. If she had been able to act, she might not have been so frightened, but she could only watch, every nerve taut, as Johnny stooped and picked up something and quickly threw it against an old drinking trough by the back door.

It fell into it with a distinct splash, and Will started, swinging in that direction, his gun held in the sighting position.

Johnny and Farmer Link ran at him together, each from a different angle, and Will gave a hoarse cry, hearing their feet crunching on the broken glass which had been flung on the yard from the windows. He whirled round, but the two men were upon him, and he crashed to the ground.

His gun went off with a noise which made the mare rise, forefeet kicking out. Sabrina was too involved with calming her for a moment to see what was happening.

When she had managed to quiet the animal, she slid down and turned to look at the struggling mass

of arms and legs which was all she could see of the
three men.

Mrs. Link was running round them, sobbing, and
little Emily stood where her mother had left her,
crouched like a wild animal, her shawl drawn up to
her mouth.

Sabrina ran to her and pushed her out of the
yard. "Go and hide behind the byre," she told her.
"Run, Emily! Run! Your mother will come for you
in a little while!"

The child obeyed, running in a clumsy, stumbling
fashion, falling over her nightgown's trailing folds.

Sabrina turned back. "Go to Emily," she told Mrs.
Link briskly. "She is by the byre. I think you should
go to her."

"My husband," sobbed Mrs. Link, "Will Duckett
shot him when they began fighting . . . I can see
blood on his nightshirt . . . The chest . . . he is shot
in the chest."

"You must go to Emily," Sabrina ordered. "You
can do nothing here, but Emily is frightened . . .
Emily needs you now . . ."

The woman ran heavily out of the yard, sobbing,
and Sabrina turned her attention to the fighting men.

They seemed to be getting nowhere in their struggle, their arms flailing wildly. She saw Will's woollen
cap under Johnny's coat sleeve and snatched up a
broken fence pole which lay near the outhouse. She
watched for the cap to emerge again from the melee,
aimed, and struck down violently.

The pole caught Farmer Link's shoulder, as he
pushed upwards suddenly. He fell backwards,
Johnny was knocked to one side, and Will Duckett

scrambled up out of the tangle, breathing heavily.

He saw Sabrina's weapon, snatched it out of her limp hands, and, so angry now that he was unaware of what he did, brought it down across her head.

She felt a sharp pain, an ache which drowned all other consciousness, and then nothing.

CHAPTER ELEVEN

She recovered consciousness in her own bedroom at Ambreys. She was aware of being awake, and yet reluctant to open her eyes because a dead weight seemed to weigh them down. Johnny's voice brought her lids fluttering up, only to close again at once in protest against the stabbing pain inflicted by the intrusion of bright daylight.

"She is waking up!" Was that his voice again, brightened by relief? The pain was growing worse, and she could not be sure. She wanted to open her eyes again to see but was too afraid of that sharp insistent agony to do so. Weakly, she moved her hand and felt the silky texture of the bed cover under her open palm. Then a hand covered hers, warmly, protectively, and she recognized the shape and feel of his strong fingers and felt a peaceful easing of her pain.

"I think we need not send," he was saying. "I think she is coming out of her unconscious state. Wait another twelve hours, Mr. Wilton, and we will see. If she recognizes one of us by then, she will be out of danger."

Her uncle's voice replied, anxious, stern. "I hope I am a Christian, but Will Duckett deserved his end for this alone . . ."

At the name, a flicker of memory troubled her. She frowned weakly and tried once more to open her eyes. Mistily, she saw Johnny bending over her, smiling, and at his shoulder, her uncle.

She tried to speak. "Johnny . . . Will Duckett . . ." the words were drawn out of her mouth like mist and wreathed away, inaudibly.

"What does she say?" asked Uncle Matthew. "What was it she said? Did you understand her, Graham?"

Her lids had fallen once more beneath the torture of the light. She strained to hear Johnny's answer.

"No, but I believe she knew me," he said cheerfully. "I am sure she knew me. Her brain may not be affected, sir. We must hope."

She was too weary to maintain her hold on conscious thought. She felt herself slipping away into the darkness of sleep and, with a sigh, relinquished her hold.

When she awoke next, Johnny was still there, sitting on a chair beside her bed, her wrist in his fingers, staring at her face. As her eyes flicked open, he smiled at her, "Good morning! You look much better today."

The pain seemed easier. She smiled back, content to see him. "Hello, Johnny."

His smile grew broader. "So you know me? That is good. How do you feel?"

She considered the question. "My head hurts," she said, and had no energy to ask questions or talk much more. All that she wanted was to fall back into sleep. Now that the pain had eased, she was snug, warm, contented. She did not want to think. She did not want to come back to ordinary life.

Johnny laid her hand back on the bed and just gently touched the fingers. "Sleep is all the medicine you need now," he said, softly. Through the gathering blur of her mind, she heard the words and smiled.

She next woke at night. When her eyes opened, there was grateful shadow around her, and by the wall a dim flicker of a candle shaded by an open book. On the chair beside it sat Charity, her head drooping down on her chest, her hands lying upward in her lap. Sabrina watched her for some moments with tenderness. There were new lines around her sister's mouth, even in sleep, which spoke to her of anxiety for her sake, pain and suffering born of love.

The door opened, and the draught made the candle flame waver. Charity woke with a start and turned her head. Into the faint circle of light stepped Aunt Maria, very softly. Her glance rested on Sabrina, and her face was gentle.

"You are awake again! How do you feel?"

Charity sprang up and came to the bed, her face glowing with delight. "Sabrina!" Her hands clasped her sister's; she bent to kiss her warmly on the cheek. "Sabrina!"

Sabrina smiled. "You do not look well, Charity. I hope I have not given you too much anxiety."

Aunt Maria answered, her voice less tender than her look, "We will speak of that when you are quite well, Sabrina. For the moment, all that matters is that you get back your strength. You look quite worn. You have eaten nothing for four days. Will you take a glass of milk or some beef tea? We have had it ready for hours. It can easily be reheated in a moment."

"Thank you," she said, "the beef tea would be delicious. I am quite hungry."

Aunt Maria went out, and Sabrina looked at Charity. "My aunt is angry with me," she said flatly.

Charity's glance did not quite meet hers. "She has been most anxious, most concerned, during your illness. She has sat up with you herself for several nights. Nobody could be more considerate."

"But she is angry with me," Sabrina insisted.

Charity sighed. "She feels you should not have gone off to look for Will Duckett alone at night. And, Sabrina, she is quite right. It was very foolhardy. See what it has brought you to! You might have been killed when he struck you. We all thought you must die when you lay there, unmoving, for hour upon hour."

"If I had come to Ambreys with the news, my uncle would have hunted the poor man down like an animal . . ."

"He deserved it . . ."

"He was sick in his mind, unhinged by his misfortunes . . ."

"He nearly killed you. He burned down Sweet Briars . . ."

"Did it burn down? Was nothing saved?" Sabrina's eyes watched her urgently.

Charity shook her head. "Nothing."

"And . . ." Sabrina was afraid to ask, "Will Duckett?"

"He ran into the house," Charity said, in a hushed whisper. "He died in the flames . . ." She broke off with a cry of remorse as she saw Sabrina wince. "Oh, I should not have told you! Dr. Graham warned me . . . I meant not to tell you . . . Oh, I am sorry, Sabrina, the shock . . . so bad for you . . ."

Sabrina drew herself together, aching suddenly with weariness, "No, no, I had to know. Poor man." She yawned, "Poor man." She was suddenly very cold, and shivered violently. "Oh . . . it is cold . . . is the window open, Charity?" She had the strangest sensation of floating, as if her bed had suddenly risen off the ground.

Charity was staring at her, frowning anxiously. "Oh, dear . . ." she heard her say.

Dimly she was aware that Charity was piling more blankets onto the bed. Their warmth seemed to reach her vaguely. She trembled in a convulsive way, her teeth chattering. "So cold," she kept saying, "so cold . . ."

People were talking, too loudly, she wanted to ask them to go away, but her throat seemed to have closed up, and she could see nothing in the darkness which surrounded her. If I could only get warm, she thought. Why does nobody light the fire? It is like December in here . . .

Then Johnny was there, lifting her up, a beaker in his hand, forcing her lips apart. A pungent liquid trickled over her tongue. She swallowed, shuddering.

Then oblivion overtook her.

She opened her eyes again to bright sunlight and the smell of hot beef tea. Aunt Maria was beside the bed, a tray in her hands.

"You look much better," she said, helping her to

sit up. She sat beside the bed and watched Sabrina drink her beef tea.

It was hot, pungent, delicious, and her stomach contracted with hunger as it reached there. She was suddenly aware of intense pleasure. Life looked very good to her, for no reason; she wanted to smile at everybody.

Aunt Maria returned her broad beam with a somewhat reserved glance. "Doctor Graham will be here soon," she said. "Are you well enough to get up? You must wash and change that nightgown. While I make the bed, try a short walk . . ."

It was surprising how quickly the body became weak. She found it very hard to stand up and even harder to walk. Her legs crumpled beneath her weight. She felt limp and lightheaded; like a rag doll she trailed herself the few short steps to the wash stand, dabbed at her face with the warm water steaming there, changed her gown, and was highly relieved to crawl back into bed afterwards.

Johnny came in, behaved with impeccable formality in Aunt Maria's watchful presence, congratulated her on her returning health, declared her much better, and left.

Aunt Maria followed him. Charity came in her stead and sat with her, sewing and talking. Then she read some of Byron's poems aloud, while Sabrina lay back, dreamily content.

She did not allow thoughts of the fire or of Will Duckett to penetrate the tissue of her thoughts. She concentrated on more cheerful ideas and was easy.

Johnny did not come to see her the next day. She

did not ask for him. He was probably very busy. He would come tomorrow.

She awoke with a feeling of trembling anticipation. He would come today. She would see him, conscious of a healing of the breach between them. The fire had, she was certain, burned out the old hostility. She had become aware of a softening in his attitude. Hope had rekindled.

However, the day wore on, and he did not come, so towards evening, she asked Charity if he were busy.

"Did you not know? He has gone to London," said Charity, her eyes carefully not meeting Sabrina's gaze. She had increasingly seemed to suspect her sister's interest in him.

Sabrina controlled an urge to cry out. "Why?" she asked.

"His brother is on the point of death, I understand, poor young man," Charity said gently. "Doctor Graham went to London to arrange a journey to Switzerland." She sighed. "Of course, he has expected it, but no doubt he feels it now the moment is upon him."

Sabrina lay back, both saddened and relieved. "Yes," she said, very softly. "Poor young man! It must be very sad to die so far away from home and family, in a strange country." But uppermost in her mind was the hope of Johnny's return. The first shock of hearing that he had left Ambresbury without informing her had given her a bitter and blinding impression of separation, total and cruel. He must have received the summons to Switzerland suddenly to have gone without visiting her to say goodbye, but

perhaps he had not wished to disturb her while she
was still weak.

Louisa came in to see her next morning, dressed
in traveling clothes, very smart and lively. She
looked at Sabrina with casual indifference. "Well,
Sabrina, how are you?" And, without awaiting an
answer, "I have come to say goodbye."

"Goodbye?" Sabrina stared, not comprehending.

"Yes, I am off to Scotland to stay with Jamie for
two months. Is not that exciting? There are to be
balls, dinners, all manner of fun. I am quite looking
forward to it, I assure you!"

Sabrina answered with what pretense of interest
she could, her whole mind secretly absorbed in
digesting the significance of this sudden departure.
Did it mean that Aunt Maria had given up hope of
Johnny for her daughter? Or was it only that, during
his absence in Switzerland, she was sending Louisa
to Scotland as a form of insurance?

From Louisa she gained no inkling of what lay
behind her visit. Louisa was totally absorbed in the
details of her Scottish trip. Lochs, mountains, crofts
and ghillies jostled with each other on her tongue.

Her mother came in to call her downstairs. Louisa
said brightly, "Well, goodbye, Sabrina! I will write
to tell you all how I enjoy my visit!" And with a
whirl of her full skirts, she was gone from the room.

The days passed very quietly. Sabrina was allowed
up out of bed, was soon walking downstairs and
spending her time quietly in the morning room with
Charity, sewing petticoats for the poor or mending
little Victoria's dresses. Several times Victoria came
out to walk with them in the shrubberies, chattering

of her sister's gaiety in Scotland. She had more importance now that she was the only child left under her family roof, and she was conscious of it. Her mother had more time for her, was constantly in the nursery, and tried to please her with gifts of new dresses and pretty velvet slippers.

Apart from meals, Sabrina saw little of Aunt Maria. When they did meet, it was in an atmosphere of coolness. Something was weighing on her aunt, clearly, and Sabrina was anxious to avoid the occasion when at last Aunt Maria would give vent to her feelings. The peaceful atmosphere of Ambreys soothed her in these trying days while Johnny was in Switzerland. She wanted nothing to disturb them.

But she was forced, in the end, to listen to Aunt Maria. One afternoon Uncle Matthew inadvertently mentioned Johnny, saying that he would now be too rich to act as village doctor and would be going away to his new estates. "We must be looking out for another fellow," he said. "I do not like these changes! The older I get, the less I like change. I can't think why, but it disturbs me."

Later, Aunt Maria came into the morning room and found Sabrina alone. Charity was in the nursery helping Victoria make a dress for one of her dolls. Sabrina looked up, startled, and, seeing her aunt's set face, knew that the moment she had been avoiding was upon her.

"So here you are," Aunt Maria began, closing the door behind her with a bang that sounded ominous in Sabrina's ears.

"Yes, Aunt?" Sabrina's voice was dry and uneasy.

"It must be said," Aunt Maria began, holding herself stiff and erect, her face a hard red in which her eyes sparkled like jet. "Your uncle, it seems, will not do it, so the duty falls upon me ... I see no good reason why you should escape scot free after your disgraceful behavior. A bump on the head does not excuse you!"

Sabrina sighed unhappily. She had heard too many of these lectures in the past.

"Oh, you may sigh! Unaccountable ... How you could behave so ... Supposed to be well brought up ... Your uncle is forever telling us what a religious man your Papa was ... I see no signs of it in his daughter, I may say! All our friends knowing. Talking of it behind our backs. Do you think Link held his tongue? Everyone for miles around hearing of it ... I am ashamed to sit in our pew on a Sunday."

"Aunt, I ..."

"Do not interrupt," cried Aunt Maria, panting, and rushed on in the same disconnected, furious voice. "Riding about with him, at such an hour ... our niece, at night with a man, like a village slut! I suppose you hoped to compromise him, make him marry you!"

The insult made Sabrina flush darkly and open her mouth to protest, but her aunt swept on over her words.

"But you chose the wrong man, Miss. Doctor Graham is not the man to be fooled by such a cheap trick!" She gave her a fierce, bitter look. "Though you have driven him away, which is what I can never forgive! He will not return! I saw it by his manner when he said goodbye, so embarrassed and red in the face, never meeting our eyes. Your wild antics have made him think again of any connection with *our* family!" She paused, her lips tightening. "Most unfair. Poor Louisa! And to think we took you into Ambreys out of the kindness of our hearts . . . a black day for us, Miss, that you ever crossed our threshold! From the first you were husband-hunting. First my Tom, then Mr. Johnstone, and then, out of spite and envy, you fixed upon Dr. Graham, to cheat poor Louisa! Oh, never shake your head at me. I know you!" She drew breath loudly, threw Sabrina a last angry glare, and left the room in a bustle of skirts, having said all she had come to say.

Sabrina stared at the closed door, her thoughts tormented. Was it true? Had all her bright dreams been mere moonshine? Did Johnny mean never to return? It was true Johnny had not come to say goodbye to her. He had left her no message, made no effort to see her. Was that his real intention? To vanish from her life again and never return? Was Aunt Maria's reading of the situation correct?

She stared across the room at the whirling golden motes of dust trapped in a warm beam of sunlight. They danced before her eyes tauntingly. What should she do if he did not come back? How was she to bear her life?

She lay awake that night, schooling herself to admit the finality of this parting, lecturing herself on the necessity to fill her life with action, to be busy and involved with life so that pain might be, if not defeated, at least numbed.

Within a week, she had permission to drive down to the village. Molly greeted her with tears and sobbed regrets for the pain her father had inflicted upon her.

Hugging her, Sabrina said, "My dear, it was not his fault. He was ill with despair. I do not blame him. And you must not do so, either."

This, for some reason, only made Molly cry harder, and at last it ended with their both drinking tea and crying together, though for very different reasons.

The village, far from treating her with the disgust her aunt had led her to believe they would show, seemed pleased and happy to see her. They came, all day, with flowers and fruit, as if to an invalid, bobbing little curtsies or nodding their heads, their speech bluntly kind. None of them mentioned the fire or Will Duckett, yet she saw the thought in each one's face, and felt a glow, as if approval wrapped her round. Whatever the county people, Aunt Maria's society friends, might think, she began to feel that the village did not condemn her, even that they were pleased with what she had tried to do.

Rob was still living in the loft over Johnny's stables. He came over to see her, as bright as ever, the shadow of his father's death already lifting from his spirit. Only a faint sadness which came down when he was not talking gave any clue to what had happened.

She moved into her cottage entirely two days later. Uncle Matthew seemed half relieved, half sad, to see her go, and drove her down himself, in the carriage. Aunt Maria came formally to say goodbye, her manner stiff. She did not kiss her nor smile, and the interview was brief.

Sabrina was sad to feel how relieved she was to leave Ambreys. She had come there with such high hopes, and now they all lay blasted. Charity, only, was sincerely unhappy at her going. She wept and begged to be allowed to come, too, but Sabrina gently refused.

"Aunt Maria will be lonely without Louisa or Tom. You will be company for her."

"But she is so unkind about you . . ."

"Then never mention me. Do not let me come between you. She is kind to you, isn't she?"

"Oh, always," Charity admitted, "but . . ."

"You will be happy here when I am away," Sabrina insisted. "Be patient, Charity."

Byrd had sent her flowers once, but he had not come to visit her. She knew that he had entirely given up all thought of her. Once or twice, Charity had mentioned seeing him at church, and then her face had glowed with soft devotion. Sabrina hoped that in time they would come together. For that to happen, Charity must meet him, and she would not do so while she was always with Sabrina herself. When Sabrina had gone from Ambreys, Byrd might visit there again.

School opened in the autumn after the gathering of the harvest. The harvest suppers were the high point of the farming year. The children, as well as the adults, attended them, and their aftereffects were felt for days, so that it was a full week after harvest supper that Sabrina opened the school.

Her pupils were rough, noisy, slow to learn, but as the days passed, she began to gain an insight into their thinking, and was able to see them making headway, and this lifted her spirits quite considerably.

One boy, a thickset, scowling lad, proved unexpectedly clever, and as he rapidly learned to read and write, and began to stretch his mind in all directions, asking more questions than she could ever find time to answer, she suddenly understood the joy of teaching.

Her quiet firmness and gentleness at first led to some bad behavior, a testing of her will, which exhausted and depressed her, but she forced herself to be patient, and gradually a working rhythm established itself.

These children wanted to learn, and that was half the battle. She saw their faces intent and curious as they followed what she said, and she delighted in making their eyes glow with amazement, or their mouths form round O's of disbelief at what she told them.

She was not content merely to teach them the rudiments of reading and writing. She wanted them to learn to use these for their further education later. She wanted to open their minds to all the wonders around them.

When she first read poetry to them, they were restless, a little scornful, almost uneasy, as if they feared they were being mocked. Poetry to them was silly, the occupation of ladies and gentlemen, of no use in the modern world. But their attitude changed when she read to them from Wordsworth and Coleridge, and soon they were as eager to hear poetry as to hear fairy stories or tales of travel and adventure.

They loved to talk of the railway and wanted to hear how it worked, what were the principles involved. She laughed, shaking her head. "I am not a scientist! But I will find out and tell you!" And, in procuring the necessary works and studying them, she realized that she was as much the pupil as the teacher and was already learning from them, as they from her.

So full and happy were her days that she barely realized how long it was since she last saw Johnny. Only at night, in her tiny bedroom, did she have the leisure to think of him, and then she strove to keep her thoughts from that subject, afraid of the depression which always followed in their wake.

Her uncle called on her several times, and Mrs. Fraser, the Vicar's wife, came often, a little pompous, as if she felt her own charity in visiting a girl so disgraced as Sabrina, but all the same welcome in that she was a great gossip and told Sabrina much that she might otherwise never know.

It was from Charity, however, that she learned that Louisa was to marry Jamie. She was so surprised that for a moment she could say nothing. Then, "Are you serious? Can it be possible?" The idea seemed ludicrous as she thought of Jamie's views on the sort of wife he desired.

Charity assured her that it was true. "They are to travel down together in a few weeks. The wedding is to follow within a month. They wish to have it before the beginning of Advent."

"And is Aunt Maria happy at the prospect?" asked Sabrina, smiling.

"Very, I believe. Ambreys is in an uproar. There has been no talk of anything else since the letter arrived."

"Well, I am happy for Louisa, but I cannot believe in this match. The young man has a Roman nature, stern and demanding. What can he have seen in Louisa to make her fit his idea of a suitable bride, I wonder?"

"Perhaps they fell in love," Charity said simply. "I suppose most people have an ideal which they never find. We must all make compromises."

Sabrina looked sharply at her. "You sound cynical today."

Charity flushed. "I? Of course not."

"I wonder if Aunt Maria had this in mind when she sent Louisa to Scotland?" Sabrina mused. "It is an excellent match on both sides. And people do like to keep their money within the family. Perhaps Jamie's family brought pressure to bear upon him. He certainly has a strong notion of family responsibility."

"I found him a very admirable and pleasant young man," said Charity.

Sabrina hugged her. "Oh, you will never see any wrong in anybody! Have you been very lonely since I left Ambreys? Have you had any visitors?"

Charity glanced down at her hands, "Mr. Johnstone has ridden over twice this week—I rode in the forest with him yesterday. He is teaching me to gallop."

Sabrina carefully suppressed any sign of triumph. Nothing would more surely embarrass her sister than to let her see that her feelings for Byrd had been penetrated. "Really? And how do you enjoy that?" she asked casually.

Charity was flushed. "Very much," she said. "The

forest is very pretty in the autumn. The many different colors of the leaves and the berries . . ."

When she had gone, Sabrina felt extremely lonely. It was only on Sunday mornings that she saw Charity now. They had fallen into the habit of walking back from church together and drinking tea for an hour until Uncle Matthew's carriage came past and picked Charity up to take her home. Uncle Matthew always remained behind for some time on Sunday to talk to the Vicar, so that Charity caused him no inconvenience.

But on Sunday afternoons, Sabrina was alone, without employment, and with only her own four walls to contemplate. Then the future, gray and featureless, pressed in upon her. Molly had leave each Sunday to walk out with Rob, through the lanes, until tea time, and the cottage seemed unbearably empty.

Sabrina stood at the window, staring out at the mild autumn afternoon, her spirits very low. She sighed, shook herself and returned to the fire. On her chair lay a volume of Byron's poems. She seated herself and opened it with a snap. She would not allow herself to brood!

Her eyes moved over the words without absorbing their meaning. The fire seemed too hot. She moved her chair back a little. Then she decided she was thirsty and went into the kitchen to fetch a glass of water. Restless, unhappy, bored, she could not settle to any occupation.

She returned to her chair and once more began to read, forcing herself to concentrate.

When the kitchen door clicked open, she looked

round in surprise, expecting to see Molly returned early from her walk. But it was Johnny who stood there, wearing a heavy traveling coat, his serious face turned towards her intently.

The book dropped from her hands. She gazed in joy and disbelief.

"Well," he said, smiling now, "I am not a ghost! Am I not to be asked to come in?"

She laughed, babbling a little, "Yes, of course, yes, please, come in . . . When did you get back?"

"Just this moment," he said, shedding his coat and walking towards her.

"You must be hungry after your journey," she said, jumping up. "I will fetch you some food . . ." Now that he was here she was painfully shy, unable to look at him, afraid that his presence did not mean what she so desperately wanted it to mean.

He caught her shoulders as she tried to slip past. "Sabrina!" he murmured, laughing.

She sighed as their lips met, then flung her arms up around his neck, clinging, without pretense of modesty, her happiness too intense to be disguised or forced down.

"Now I know I have come home," he said, drawing back after a moment, and touched her cheek with one finger, half teasing, half loving. "Will you marry me, Sabrina? As I came home, the very wheels seemed to be asking that . . . Will Sabrina marry me? And it galled me beyond measure to have to wait so long to discover the answer."

She smiled, shivered, half withdrew. "Oh, Johnny, how can I, when you still believe me capable . . ."

"No," he said quickly, silencing her with his finger, "no, I know the truth, now, Sabrina. When I saw my uncle, I told him I was going to ask you to marry me; I told him I would not have this cloud hanging over you any longer, that I no longer believed what he had told me . . ."

"Oh," she said, against his finger, her eyes on his face, her lips curving up into a smile of delight.

He gave her a glance of tender affection. "During these months, everything you have said or done has made me conscious of a disparity between what you were and what my uncle claimed of you. I saw you act impulsively, foolishly, bravely. I never saw you commit a mean or deceitful act once. You were too open, too honest, too direct, if anything. And I was forced to ask myself how such a girl could have deliberately made love to two men at once, fostered a secret and illicit affair with a married man, lied and cheated in her personal relationships! It was not possible. The only answer was that the facts were wrong. I no longer believed you capable of acting in such a fashion. My uncle, on the other hand, I knew to be a man quite capable of lying."

Her eyes asked a question, and he smiled grimly. "He told me, when I first informed him I was coming to Ambresbury, that you had married."

"Married?" she repeated incredulously.

"Yes. He suspected, I think, that I chose this village because you had several times mentioned it as being close to the home of your own uncle." He grinned at her, mischievously, "And I might as well confess, now, that some such thought was in my head. Not that I hoped or wished to marry you then, or even meet you again, but some lingering attrac-

tion must have given an allure to this place as being
familiar to you. But when my uncle heard of my
decision, he at once, voluntarily, told me that he
had heard you were married. I believed him, of
course, but when I met you again, I found his infor-
mation to be inaccurate. I did not think much of it
at the time—I assumed he had been wrongly informed. Later, my ideas changed."

"What did he say when you taxed him with lying?" she asked.

"He was angry. He blustered and shouted for a
time, but when it became clear that I was immov-
able, he tried to coax me into good humor. His manner was proof of my suspicions—he reddened when
I first mentioned you, and was both aggressive and
uncertain. Eventually, I forced him to admit that he
had lied, that he had forced his attentions on you
that one evening, that you had been utterly truthful
throughout . . ."

"But why? Why did he lie?" she asked in
bewilderment.

"Because he wished to part us—he knew I loved
you, he was determined I should not marry you. The
match was not good enough in his eyes, you had no
money and no friends. He leaped at the chance of
discrediting you. It was all very carefully planned. It
seems my aunt was in the plot, too—she brought me
back at the right moment, and they had timed his
attack upon you so that I should see you so com-
promised that I would never forgive it."

"Good God," she said, "to go to such lengths!"

"It was shameful," he agreed. "We parted on no
very good terms. I hope never to see either of them

again. When I think of the cruel, bitter things I have said to you, my jealousy and hostility . . . I shall never forgive them."

She could not pretend to disagree.

He drew her closer again. "Let us forget them. Will you marry me, then, Sabrina? Can you forgive me? Before I had forced the confession out of my uncle, I had decided I could not live without you—that was why I left you that note."

"What note?" she asked in a puzzled voice.

His brows drew together. "Did you not receive it? I left it with your aunt. You were asleep, and I did not wish to disturb you at such a late hour."

"She did not give it to me," she said, understanding now why Aunt Maria had been so angry. She must have read it and then destroyed it.

Johnny grimaced. "We are both unfortunate in our relatives," he said dryly. "Well, my love, we must form our own family and shut out the rest of the world. What do you say?"

Her happiness made her tremble, but she managed to say, "Yes."

He held her, kissing her passionately on the mouth, one hand on her hair. "In my vanity, I had persuaded myself you loved me, but I could not be absolutely certain. I thought I must be right that night in the forest when you came into my arms so naturally. How your Aunt Maria would have stared in horror!"

"Yes," she said, severely, "you are very conceited . . ."

He kissed her again, hard and briefly. "Dancing

Hill has stood empty too long. We will fill it with life again."

She smiled. "I dread to consider what reaction we shall receive from my aunt."

"She will learn to live with the idea," he dismissed, "and we shall take the Ducketts with us—there is a cottage at the lodge gate which will do nicely for them."

"Oh, yes, let us do something for the Ducketts! Will they allow them all to leave the Workhouse?"

"Of course," he said calmly, "they will be glad to be rid of such a large charge on the rates. I suppose they never caught Will Duckett's accomplices? I have had no news since I left."

She shook her head, "No, Mr. Link could not identify them. They were never found."

They sat down together by the fire and talked softly of the future. "Charity will live with us, of course," he said. "We shall be beginning our married life with a family!"

"I have hopes of Byrd Johnstone for her," she told him, with a smile.

"What?" he exclaimed, laughing.

"He needs a wife," she said airily, "and he certainly could not find a better one!"

"Well, do not ask me to like the fellow," said Johnny, with a grin. "He caused me too much jealousy. I shall never forget that day by the river. I was so afraid you would marry him, and it was that day which made me admit to myself that I still loved you."

She leaned over to kiss him. "I could not have

married him. And he never loved me, you know. I could not hurt him by my refusal since his emotions were never involved."

"The man is a bigger fool than I had supposed," he declared. "How could he help not loving you?"

She shook her head, smiling.

Later she sobered, "Your poor brother . . . I am so sorry, my love. I have not expressed my sympathy. It is very sad . . ."

"Yes," he said, his expression altering, "I was not in time to say my last farewell to him. I felt that."

"He had a sad life," she said, "so much illness . . ."

"Yes. Lately he has often written to me of his desire to think of Dancing Hill in use once more as a family home, with children and horses, just as it was when we were children. I wish I had been able to tell him about you. I know he would have been glad to hear we were to marry."

She held his hand tightly, and they were silent for a while.

"Who is going to tell Aunt Maria?" she murmured after a while, and he had the grace to look a little red.

"Oh, I think it would come best from you," he said, laughing.

"Coward! But Louisa's engagement will soften the blow," she said, slyly glancing at him.

He started. "What?"

She told him, laughing, "So you need not tremble! You are safe from Louisa!"

"Your aunt's scheming more than once caused me grave embarrassment, Miss," he said severely, then rose and pulled her up out of her chair. "Do you realize I have not kissed you for quite ten minutes? I hope this is not how you intend to conduct yourself in married life? I shall expect my kisses, like my meals, at regular and frequent intervals!"

She was not sorry to obey.

OTHER FICTION
FROM
PLAYBOY PRESS

THE DRAGON AND THE ROSE $1.95
ROBERTA GELLIS

Henry had been hunted, betrayed and attacked by his
political enemies since the day he was born. He had
conquered his fear of the constant danger surrounding
him, but could he conquer the woman he had agreed to
wed—the woman who represented all he had learned to
despise, the one who would profit most from his death?
Beautiful, passionate and clever, Elizabeth had been
born of royal blood and possessed the arrogance and
self-control of a queen. Forced by her mother to marry
a man she abhorred, she went to her marriage bed with
head held high and a heart filled with fear.

ROSELYNDE $1.95
ROBERTA GELLIS

In an era made for men, Alinor is at no man's mercy.
Beautiful, proud and strong-willed, she is mistress of
Roselynde and her own heart as well—until she meets
Simon, the battle-scarred knight appointed to be her
warden, a man whose passion and wit match her own.
Their struggle to be united against all obstacles sweeps
them from the pageantry of the Royal Court to a dar-
ing Crusade through exotic Byzantium and into the
Holy Land. The first book of the magnificent medieval
romantic saga, THE ROSELYNDE CHRONICLES.

ALINOR $2.25
ROBERTA GELLIS

A woman alone . . . trapped in a deadly maze of
treacherous power plays and volatile liaisons, Alinor
Lemagne is irresistibly swept into an intoxicating,
breathless passion for the darkly sensual man whose
forbidden love promises only pain and peril. Swirling
from the bloody battlegrounds of France and England
to the rich pageantry of the king's court, her passionate
adventures weave a breathtaking tale of danger and
desire—and a beautiful woman's desperate quest for
love.

LOVE'S GENTLE FUGITIVE $1.95
ANDREA LAYTON

A runaway to the New World, ravishingly beautiful Elizabeth Bartlett tries to escape her secret past—only to learn that shame and degradation are the price for her freedom. Frightened and vulnerable, she is rescued from brutal slavery by the one man who could return her to England and disaster. On a brave journey through the wilderness, she succumbs to irresistible temptation and falls deeply in love with the handsome, bold protector who has aroused her most turbulent yet tender emotions. As their surging desires find release in rapturous ecstasy, Elizabeth surrenders her heart—and her destiny—to the passionate stranger who could choose to love her . . . or betray her.

THE SCANDALOUS LADY $1.50
MAGGIE GLADSTONE

As one of the dazzling Lacebridge belles, Sara was expected to marry a man of wealth and position. Instead she scandalized all polite society by running away to pursue her dream of stardom on the London stage. There she set out to prove her worth, never dreaming that she would capture the heart of Covent Garden's most handsome and sought-after leading man. The first in a series of four delightful regency romances.

THE SWORD AND THE SWAN $1.95
ROBERTA GELLIS

Rannulf was known throughout the land as a bold warrior. Face-to-face with an oncoming army, he could decide matters of life and death. But now, face-to-face with one gentle woman, he was hopelessly confused and uncertain. Startled by Catherine's pale beauty when he first saw her, he was dumbfounded by her passionate radiance now, and he felt a desire far different from his usual impersonal need for a woman.